Shortbread and Sorrow

A Peridale Cafe MYSTERY

AGATHA FROST

Other books in the Peridale Café Series

A Peridale Cafe MYSTERY

Book Five

CHAPTER I

J ulia inhaled the sweet icing as she finished piping Jessie's name onto the smooth surface of the birthday cake. She stepped back and assessed her work, unhappy with how wobbly the '*J*' looked. Mowgli, her grey Maine Coon, jumped up onto the counter and looked down disapprovingly at the cake before turning and sashaying to his food dish.

"You've missed a candle," Sue, Julia's sister, whispered over her shoulder. "There should be seventeen, and you've only put sixteen."

Julia quickly counted the candles. Her sister was right. She let out a soft chuckle, plucked a seventeenth candle from the large bag, and slotted it in a free space around the edge of the cake. Being the best baker in the small Cotswold village of Peridale meant she was often called upon late at night to quickly whip up birthday cakes for residents who didn't want to admit they had forgotten a loved one's special day. She always did her best to meet their deadlines, but when it came to family and friends, she always put a little extra love and care into the baking. She had been mentally planning Jessie's cake for weeks.

"Smells delicious," Sue said as she hovered over the cake. "Is that vanilla?"

"Just a dash," Julia said, slapping Sue's hand away before she swiped her finger along the edge. "Dot and Jessie should be back by now."

They both looked at the cat clock above the fridge as its tail and eyes darted from side to side. It was a little after midday, but it didn't surprise Julia that their gran was late. Dot worked to her own clock, which rarely synced up with anybody else's.

Julia placed the cake in the fridge and quickly wiped away the spilled flour. She dumped the dishes and whisk in the sink for washing later, and dusted the dried icing off her caramel-coloured flared dress.

"Have you got anything sweet to eat?" Sue asked as she poked through Julia's fridge. "I've been craving chocolate all week."

"Top shelf," Julia said with a soft smile as she reached around Sue to grab a plastic tub. "Plenty of chocolate cake left over. I know it's Barker's favourite, but I think I've made it so much that he's sick to death of it."

As though he had heard his name, a key rattled in the front door, and Barker hurried into the cottage, still in his work suit. He dropped his briefcase by the door, hung his sand-coloured trench coat on the hat stand, and checked his reflection in the hallway mirror, tweaking his dark hair slightly. Sue and Julia looked at each other and smirked.

"You've given him a key?" Sue mumbled through a mouthful of cake. "You two must be getting serious."

Julia blushed. Barker had moved to the village nearly four months ago to fill the vacant Detective Inspector position at the local police station. They hadn't started out on the best terms, but they had been dating for over three months now, and they were very much in love. The exchanging of front door keys had happened two weeks ago, and at the time, Julia had not thought it was a big step, mainly because they were both getting tired of having to knock on each other's doors whenever they wanted to see each other. From the amused look on her sister's face, she was beginning to wonder if she had missed a relationship milestone that was a big deal to other people. Julia promptly dismissed the thought. Ever since their first meeting, her relationship with Barker had been anything but conventional.

"Am I late?" Barker asked as he kissed Julia softly on the cheek, his greying stubble brushing against her soft skin and his spicy cologne tickling her nostrils. "Is that *my* chocolate cake you're eating, Sue?"

"You can have some if you like," Sue said as she took another bite, cake flying from her mouth. "I've been craving chocolate."

Another key rattled in the door, signalling the arrival of Jessie and Dot, both of whom also had their own keys to Julia's cottage. She was pleased to see it was Jessie, her lodger, who was unlocking the door, and not her Gran, who had a habit of letting herself in whenever she felt like it, day or night.

"It's only us," Dot announced, just like she did every other time she entered. "I know we're late! *I know, I know*! But there was a tractor driving up the lane, and the taxi couldn't get through. Hello, girls."

"Hello, Gran," Julia and Sue replied in unison.

"Barker," Dot said with a curt nod, dropping her shopping bags by the door before adjusting the brooch holding her white collar under her chin, using the same mirror Barker had used to play with his hair. "Aren't you supposed to be at work fighting crime and not scoffing cake?"

"It's my lunch break," Barker mumbled through some of the cake Sue had shared with him.

Julia looked down at the shopping bags Jessie was holding. She had a huge grin on her face, and Julia was surprised to see she was still wearing the '*Seventeen Today!*' badge that Dot had insisted she put on before she took her out for a birthday shopping spree.

"I don't remember getting that much stuff on my seventeenth birthday," Sue murmured in Julia's ear.

"Times have *changed*!" Dot exclaimed as she waved her hands around, her hearing as robust as ever. "The kids these days want all sorts of things that I can't quite wrap my head around. What's the point in those Apple Pad *whatchamacall them* things if you can't write on them! Not like any pad *I've* ever known."

"They have apps on them," Jessie said, reaching into one of the bags to pull out the latest model of a tablet. "And the internet, and stuff."

"That couldn't have come cheap," Barker said after an intake of breath.

"Never you mind!" Dot said, extending a finger and wagging it in Barker's face as she pushed past him. "Julia, where's your radio?"

Julia watched as Jessie sat at the counter and eagerly unwrapped the plastic off her new gadget. It warmed Julia to see the look of joy on Jessie's face, especially because she would like people to think she was just another surly-faced teenager. After a lifetime of foster care, and six months sleeping on the streets before Julia had taken her in, she knew the gifts meant much more to Jessie than she would admit. Julia had gone to great lengths to ensure every part of her first birthday in Peridale was the best she had ever had. She hadn't even minded dipping into her little pot of savings to give Dot money to buy Jessie the tablet she had been eyeing up online for weeks.

"*Radio?*" Dot exclaimed. "*Where* is it? Tony Bridges' program is coming up on *Classic Radio* any second!"

"What do you want to listen to that for, Gran?"

Sue asked, arching a brow at Julia, who could only shrug back. "Tony Bridges is *ancient*! He was on the radio back when I was a kid and he was old then."

"And me," Barker added.

"None of your business!" Dot mumbled as she ducked under the sink and rummaged through the cleaning products.

Julia reached up and grabbed the radio from the top of the fridge. She brushed off a layer of dust and handed it to Dot, who snatched it up to her face. She twiddled with the dials and buttons, lifting it up to her ear to give it a hard shake until she found the station she wanted.

"*And that was the smooth sound of Barry Manilow,*" Tony Bridges, the radio presenter, announced as the music faded out. "Coming up next we have a little Stevie Wonder, and *then* it's our daily *Music Quiz* at half past the hour!"

Dot glanced at the clock as she rested the radio on the counter, nodding her head as she counted the tiny markings on the clock. They all exchanged glances, confused and amused by her strange behaviour. Julia had never thought her gran was much of a music fan, but she knew her gran was a fickle woman who could change her habits and interests at the drop of a hat.

Remembering what she had been waiting to do all morning, Julia nudged Sue and nodded to the light switch. Sue tapped the side of her nose and scooted across the room as Julia pulled the birthday cake out of the fridge. Jessie was so distracted by her new purchase, she didn't notice Julia striking a match to quickly light all seventeen candles. Julia winked to Sue, who flicked off the lights, sending her bright kitchen into partial darkness thanks to the lingering grey clouds outside.

Julia enthusiastically led a chorus of '*Happy Birthday*' over Stevie Wonder, which grew louder and louder as Dot crammed her ear up to the speaker and cranked up the volume. Jessie blushed, pretending to be transfixed by the screen, but she was unable to contain the smirk prickling the sides of her lips.

"Make a wish," Julia announced as she set the cake on the counter.

Jessie rolled her eyes, but her smile broke free when she looked down and saw her name iced onto the cake's surface. She clenched her eyes, thought for a minute, and then blew out the candles with one swift breath. They gave her a little round of applause, which only caused Dot to turn up the radio even louder.

Shortbread and Sorrow

"What did you wish for?" Barker asked as he glared over his shoulder at Dot.

"I wished that you'd turn into a donkey," Jessie said with a small shrug. "Because you're always making an a-,"

"I *guess* you won't want this then," Barker jumped in, pulling a small envelope out of his inside pocket.

He waved it in front of Jessie's face for a second before she snatched it out of his hands and ripped it open. Instead of a birthday card, or even money, an application form fell out. Julia recognised it as a learner driver provisional license application form, although it had changed a lot since she had applied for hers at Jessie's age.

"I thought I could teach you to drive," Barker said coolly, his cheeks reddening a little. "I'll put you on my insurance once you have your provisional. In my car, of course. No offence, Julia, but I don't think I would trust your old banger to get to the end of the road with anybody else driving it but you."

Julia was too touched to be offended. Barker hated her vintage aqua blue Ford Anglia, but she would keep driving it until the wheels fell off and the engine finally died.

"You'd do that?" Jessie mumbled, dropping her

hair over her face. "Thanks."

"I like you sometimes," Barker said with a wink as he ruffled Jessie's hair. "Only *sometimes* though."

"Yeah, well it's a good job I don't like you most of the time." Jessie slapped his hand away and ducked out of the way, a small smirk on her lips.

Julia laughed, even though Sue looked a little confused by their exchange. Julia treated Jessie like she would her own daughter, and even though she was dating Barker, he was more of a brother than a father figure. They bickered and fought like siblings, but she knew they cared about each other, maybe even liked each other, not that they would admit it.

Just as Julia sliced into the cake after taking out the candles, which she would put back into her collection ready for use on another birthday cake, Dot whizzed past her, grabbing the house phone off the wall as she did. She ran across to the bathroom and slammed the door, the spiral cord on the phone almost entirely stretched out. A small laugh of disbelief escaped Julia's lips.

"She's nuts," Jessie said. "She bought me new Doc Martens too. I told her she didn't have to."

Julia smiled because she knew they had been bought with Dot's own money. She sat next to Jessie and watched as she tapped away on the tablet, installing various apps and games.

"What's she doing in there?" Sue whispered, glancing over at the bathroom door.

"Do you really want to know?" Barker asked.

They both stared at each other for a moment before snickering like naughty school children. Julia picked up a piece of the sliced cake and took a small bite. Just as she suspected, the sponge was light and fluffy, and the icing was delicate and sweet. Even by her impossibly high standards, it was almost perfect.

"There's something I want to tell you when Gran gets back," Sue murmured, chewing the inside of her lip.

"*Oh*?" Julia asked, a brow arching.

Sue opened her mouth to speak as she looked down at her fumbling fingers, but before any words came out, Dot's voice filled the kitchen.

"*Hello? Am I on?*"

Julia turned to the bathroom door, as did Jessie, but Sue and Barker turned to the radio on the counter.

"*You're through to Tony Bridges' music quiz,* where *you* can win a holiday for *you* and *two* of your friends, granted that *you* get the answer right!" Tony exclaimed jollily through the speakers. "Tell us your name and where you're from."

"Oh my God, I'm *actually* through," Dot cried through the phone, loud enough that Julia could hear her on both ends. "Do you know how many times I've tried to get on this stupid show? *Every day* for two *whole* weeks! *Two*! I was about to give up!"

There was an awkward pause on the radio and in the room. Sue hurried over and turned up the volume as she cast a curious look over her shoulder to Julia.

"Yeah, well, *a lot* of people try to get on the air," Tony said with an uncomfortable laugh. "My producer tells me your name is *Dorothy* and you're from Peri – Perimale?"

"It's *Dot*," she snapped harshly. "And it's *Peridale*. What's the question? I don't have time for niceties. I want to win the holiday!"

There was another awkward silence as Sue and Julia both cringed. Julia was unable to even look at the radio. She could practically see the bemused grin of the DJ in the studio as he motioned to his producer to find out who had let the crazy old woman on air.

"Well, it seems we have ourselves a firecracker here, ladies and gents," Tony joked. "It's a good job I like them lively. *Okay,* folks, I'm going to get straight into this one. It's an easy one today. Are you ready Dot?"

"Of course I'm ready! I phoned in!"

Tony coughed and took a large intake of breath before deciding to speak.

"Okay, *here we go*! The Police spent three weeks at number one with their classic hit '*Message in a Bottle*', but in what year and month? I need *both answers* for you to win the holiday."

"She'll never get that," Sue whispered. "She doesn't know anything about pop culture."

"I think it was 1981," Barker mumbled.

"What's *The Police*?" Jessie asked.

They all turned to the seventeen-year-old and scowled, which caused Jessie to scowl right back.

"I remember hearing that song as a kid," Julia said. "But it could have been anytime in the early 1980s."

Dot cleared her throat, forcing them into silence. They turned back to the radio and listened attentively through bated breaths. She grumbled for a moment, whispering nonsensically under her breath. Julia was sure she was about to say something completely out of the blue, maybe even hang up entirely.

"I need an answer, Dorothy."

"It's *Dot*," she said through gritted teeth. "I

know it. I know it. I think it was *September* in 1979. *Yes.* That's right. I'm *sure* of it."

There was another long dramatic pause before congratulatory trumpets crackled through the speakers, surprisingly them all.

"Well I don't believe it folks, but it seems Dot has pulled this one out of the bag! That's absolutely correct. How did you know?"

"It was number one when my first granddaughter, Julia, was born," Dot said, her tone softening a little. "I remember because it was playing in the delivery room and I told one of the nurses to shut it off. Total nonsense if you ask me. Not what I'd call music."

"Well, you've won the holiday!" Tony cried as the trumpets faded out. "Would you like to find out where that nonsense is taking you?"

There was a drumroll, which echoed loudly around the small kitchen. Sue turned to Julia, an excited grin on her face as she clenched her hands against her mouth. Julia almost couldn't believe what was happening, but it was her gran, so she had stopped trying to second-guess her thought processes a long time ago.

"You've won an all-inclusive five-night stay in a luxury spa hotel on the banks of the gorgeous Loch

Shortbread and Sorrow

Lomond in Scotland!"

"*Scotland?*" Dot cried. "Bloody *Scotland?* The woman yesterday won a three-week cruise around the Bahamas. This is an *outrage!* I want to speak to your -,"

Before Dot could continue with her rant, Tony cut her off, and in turn, Sue clicked off the radio. They all turned to the bathroom door and watched as Dot shuffled out, a defeated look on her face as she mumbled bitterly to herself.

"*Scotland!*" she cried again. "Well, I suppose it's better than a kick in the teeth."

"I can't believe you just won a radio competition!" Sue squealed, pulling her gran into a tight hug. "All thanks to Julia's birth."

"Me and the girls have been trying all month! They've been calling it their *May-Cation Bonanza!* I guess they ran out of the decent holidays in the first week! The questions are *too* easy. That's their problem. And you better believe it, young lady." Dot wriggled out of the hug and adjusted her roller-set curls. "Because you're coming with me. You too, Julia."

Julia looked to Barker, and then to Jessie, and finally to her gran. Just from the look on Dot's face, it didn't seem that Julia had any choice in the matter.

"Gran, I can't," she protested. "I have the café, and the -,"

"I'll watch the café," Jessie jumped in. "I've done it before."

"And I'll make sure she doesn't burn it down," Barker added, to which Jessie stuck her tongue out at him. "I can start teaching her to drive too. It'll be fun."

"I wouldn't exactly call it *fun*," Jessie grumbled.

Julia stared at Sue, who already looked like she had her heart set on it. Julia looked down at the cake, trying to remember the last time she had been on holiday, Scotland or not. It had been a long time before she had opened her café, and that was more than two years ago. She exhaled, and her mind wandered to the list of spa treatments that would be on offer. She could feel Sue's eager eyes pleading with her to say yes, and she wasn't sure she had the heart to say no to her sister.

"I'll be able to juggle my shifts around at the hospital," Sue said as she pushed into Julia's side and rested their heads together. "*Please*, big sis. We need some girl time. It'll be fun."

"You had me at *spa*," Julia said with a defeated smile. "When do you think we should go? Next month?"

"Well it's Sunday today, and we get five nights, so we'll go to the spa on Wednesday. I'll get it all sorted on the phone, so you don't have to worry about a thing! He did say all-inclusive." Dot shuffled over to the door and picked up her shopping bags. "I must dash. I'm going to have to buy some new boots and a thick coat. Scotland is hardly the Bahamas, but that doesn't mean we can't make the most of it. Enjoy the rest of your birthday, Jessie."

Dot waved a hand and disappeared out of the door like the whirlwind she was. In her absence, they all sat in baffled silence, staring absently at the birthday cake.

"I guess we're going to Scotland," Sue laughed, shaking her head. "The home of shortbread and kilts!"

"You know they don't wear underwear under those things," Jessie mumbled through a mouthful of cake with a small shudder. "What did you want to tell us?"

Sue looked awkwardly around the kitchen, her cheeks blushing. She looked Julia dead in the eyes, and Julia could feel the fear consuming her sister. When she blinked, she appeared to push it away in an instant, glazing a fake smile over the top. She shook her curls, which would have been identical to Julia's own chocolaty curls if she didn't insist on her monthly blonde highlights. She frowned and looked down at the ground, before looking up and staring absently out of the window and into Julia's garden, just as the clouds started to clear and the sun began to peek through.

"You know what, it's slipped my mind," Sue said faintly, snapping her fingers together. "Couldn't have been important. I think I'm going to follow Gran out. Shopping is in order, and I need to make sure Neil is going to be okay by himself. You know what men are like. Enjoy the cake!"

Barely a minute after Dot had left, Sue hurried out of the cottage. Jessie and Barker didn't seem to have noticed the strange look in Sue's eye, but Julia had, and she knew for certain that whatever it had been, had been important, despite her claims of forgetting.

"Scotland," Barker whispered under his breath. "That sounds lovely. Let's all go out for lunch at The Comfy Corner. My treat. I want to spend as much time with you as I can before Dot whisks you away."

He pulled Julia in and kissed her on the side of the head. She realised she was going to miss Barker while she was away, even if it was only for five nights. Despite that, she knew Sue was right. It had been too long since they had enjoyed quality sister time together. Julia was embarrassed to say it had been months since she had really had an in-depth girls' chat with her little sister. All it would take was a glass of wine and Julia would be able to get to the bottom of her stumbled announcement.

CHAPTER 2

Relief surged through Julia when she saw a sign for the *McLaughlin Spa and Hotel*. Even though they had been driving in her tiny luggage-packed Ford Anglia for seven hours, it felt like she had been trapped in a tin can for days, no thanks to her gran's sudden and unwavering enthusiasm for her radio competition prize.

"Did I mention the hotel overlooked Loch

Lomond, which is the largest loch in Scotland by surface area?" Dot repeated again like a parrot that had swallowed an encyclopaedia. "Says in this book that it was formed ten thousand years ago at the end of the last ice age."

Julia and Sue both glimpsed at each other in the front seat. If they weren't so exhausted, they probably would have laughed at hearing the fact for the third time. She eased her car into second gear and slowed to a crawl as they entered a small village which looked like it could be Peridale's twin.

"This is Aberfoyle," Dot exclaimed enthusiastically. "It's the nearest village to the spa. According to this book, there were only eight hundred residents during the census in 2010. Do you know how many residents Peridale has, Julia?"

"I don't, Gran," Julia said, forcing a smile as she glanced at her in the rear-view mirror. "We're not far away."

"I'm going to need a spa after this drive," Sue mumbled out of the corner of her mouth. "Or maybe a nice long nap."

The thought of a nap enticed Julia. She had been in such a rush to leave that morning, she hadn't had time to enjoy her usual peppermint and liquorice tea, nor eat any breakfast. Her stomach rumbled when she looked out of the window as they passed a small café, not unlike her own. The dry sandwich at the last service station hadn't even touched the sides.

Despite her exhaustion and hunger coupled with the temptation of cake and tea, the dropping miles on her sat-nav encouraged her forward. Even if she hadn't been completely sold on the idea of a spa break at first, it was all she had been able to think about since. She had never been great at relaxing, especially when she knew there was always something that needed to be done at the café, but with Jessie taking care of things and Barker watching over her, she was ready to forget all about Peridale and spend the next couple of days with an empty mind.

They drove out of Aberfoyle and followed a small winding road up a steep grassy hill. Her poor car groaned, so she shifted gears, slammed her foot down on the accelerator, and willed it to make it over the top. When the road eventually flattened out, she knew it had been worth it.

"*Wow*," Dot whispered. "Would you look at that?"

"It's *beautiful*," Sue agreed.

The view completely stole Julia's breath. It took

all of her strength to keep her eyes on the road, and not on the sprawling green hills and misshapen loch. Small islands dotted through the water, as though they had just drifted downstream and decided they were going to settle where they were. Beautiful swathes of grey, blue, and green all mixed together, bringing to mind a murky watercolour painting where the artist had forgotten to clean their water.

"I see the hotel!" Dot cried, jumping forward and cramming her finger between the two of them. "It's *there!*"

Sue and Julia both looked to where she was pointing. Their eyes landed on a large, imposing medieval castle on one of the larger islands nearer the bank. Its pale gold stone almost blended in with the colours of the landscape, and if it wasn't for the blue and white Scottish flag flying proudly at its entrance, Julia might not have noticed it out of the corner of her eye.

"Are you sure that's it, Gran?" Julia asked as she checked the tiny map on the screen, which wasn't showing her anything beyond the winding road ahead.

"Of course I'm sure!" she snapped. "I've done my research on the place. It dates all the way back to the 13th century."

"They had spas back then?" Sue asked with a wrinkled nose.

"Of course not!" she snapped again, rolling her eyes at Julia in the rear-view mirror. "The spa was a recent addition in the last twenty years, but the castle, official title Seirbigh Castle, has been with the McLaughlin family since the 1930s. It was nothing more than a couple of ruins on an island when they bought it, but they fully restored it and gave it a purpose."

Julia spotted another sign for the hotel and almost couldn't believe her gran was right. The road took a sharp right turn, and the castle appeared in front of her. She turned to her sister, who was sharing the same look of disbelief. Julia let out a small laugh as she looked up at the grand structure. She hadn't expected much, considering it was a radio competition prize, but Seirbigh Castle had blown those low expectations right out of the water.

"This is going to be the best five days of our lives," Sue said as she took in the incredible vista. "Look at this place!"

The road narrowed, forcing Julia to slow to a snail's pace. Her car rocked as they transitioned onto the stone bridge that connected the land to the island. Dot hurriedly wound down her window and crammed her head through the gap.

"We're driving over the loch," she cried into the breeze.

"Somebody has changed their tune," Sue whispered to Julia. "I thought she wanted the Bahamas?"

"If I'd have known Scotland was so beautiful, I wouldn't have complained," Dot snapped back, her hearing not failing her once again. "The TV makes it look like an awful dreary place. If they showed more of this, people might actually want to come here."

Julia and Sue both shook their heads in unison as they dismounted the bridge and drove towards the castle. The gravel crunched under the tyres below as the crisp loch air drifted in through the open window. She inhaled, and a feeling of calm washed over her, forcing her to sink a little lower into her seat as she pulled her car into one of four empty spaces at the base of the castle entrance.

Before Julia had finished unbuckling her belt, Dot jumped out of the car and ran to the edge of the small island. She whipped a small disposable camera out of her handbag, wound it along, crammed it to her eye and started snapping the breath-taking view. Julia was sure an entire roll of film wouldn't be enough to capture the true beauty of the place.

Julia and Sue unloaded the car while their gran scuttled from spot to spot to get different angles. Julia had managed to fit all of her luggage into a single weekend bag, but her sister and gran had taken a more liberal approach to their packing, each bringing what appeared to be the entire contents of their wardrobes.

"A hat box?" Julia asked as she reached out for the oval case, arching a brow.

"I didn't know what the weather was going to be like," Sue said, snatching it out of her hand. "I bought it when me and Neil went to Moscow, and I've been trying to find an excuse to use it. I thought it would be snowing."

"It's spring."

"It's *Scotland*."

Julia laughed and shook her head. She shut the boot and locked the car before picking up as many of the bags as she could. Between them, they managed to grab everything, leaving their gran to continue her photo shoot. Before they set off up the slope towards the castle's entrance, Julia looked out at the dark loch once more, which stretched out for miles in either direction. She inhaled again as the wind licked her hair, the air moist and floral.

"*Heather*," she said to Sue, pointing to the

purple flower covering the bank around them. "It smells beautiful."

"Your baker's nose never fails you," Sue said, before turning to their gran, who was halfway back along the bridge and snapping the water below. "*Gran*! We can't check in without you."

Dot reluctantly dragged herself away and dropped her camera into her bag, not without snapping a picture of Julia and Sue first. Without offering to take any of the bags, she shuffled past them and up the slope, which wound around the side of the castle.

The entrance, which was signposted as '*McLaughlin Spa and Hotel Retreat*' in bold gold lettering, looked like any other traditional castle entrance Julia had seen. It was door-less, and tall, double any of their heights. The castle appeared to be divided into three separate buildings, all joined together like a mismatched jigsaw. Julia wasn't much of a history buff, but she was sure if she had a look at her gran's guidebook, she would read that parts of the castle were older than others, with different invasions and families adding on their own sections. The entrance, which was the simplest part of the building, appeared to also be the oldest.

Led by Dot, they walked in through the

entrance, which took them to a large ajar mahogany door. The first sign of modern civilisation was a table containing tourist leaflets next to the door. Dot picked up one of each, before yanking on the gold handle. The door creaked open, and she slipped through, letting it slam shut again. Julia shook her head, and Sue let out a long sigh. Julia dropped her bags and opened the door for Sue, who slipped in, and in turn she dropped hers and held it open for Julia.

Julia walked along the embroidered red carpet into the grand entrance hall. A matching mahogany staircase swept up the left side of the space, ending at a landing, which led off to many doors. The walls were exposed in some parts, and wood-lined in others, with heavy-framed oil paintings cluttering them in equal quantities. A large reception desk, with the spa's logo, sat at the far side of the room, with a door directly behind it leading off to what appeared to be an office. The desk was unmanned, but that didn't stop Dot from hurrying over and enthusiastically slapping the small metal bell. It rang out through the entrance hall, echoing into the corners. Julia slowly sauntered over as she attempted to take in every detail. She dropped her bags by the desk and turned to face the roaring fire that burned in the fireplace, which was as tall, if not taller, than her. It put her cottage's fireplace to shame.

Just from her first glimpse of the spa, Julia was sure she was going to enjoy it very much. She could already feel herself relaxing, and it was a feeling that she enjoyed, even if it was foreign to her. Peridale felt all of the three hundred and sixty miles away that it was, and even though she loved her little village, she was surprised how glad she was to be away.

Unfortunately for Julia, that tranquillity didn't last long. A door slammed, casting out any peaceful thoughts from her mind. She stepped back and looked up at the landing where the noise had come from. To her surprise, a black bag flew towards her, and she barely darted out of the way before it landed on the ground and split open. The plastic bag burst on impact and women's clothes, in a size much smaller and much more expensive looking than Julia's, spewed across the stone floor.

"I've told you once, and I'll tell you again!" a man's deep voice bellowed, his Scottish accent the strongest Julia had heard. "We're *over!*"

The man appeared from the door the clothes had flown out of, dragging a woman by the arm. He seemed to be in his early sixties, but slight in frame and very short. His head was completely bald and shiny and looked as though it was barely balancing on his narrow shoulders. His sharp cheekbones and sunken sockets created two shadows where his eyes should have been. The woman, on the other hand, was curvaceous and looked to be in her mid-forties. She struggled against the man's grip, but he was clearly much stronger than her despite his weak appearance. The hairs on Julia's neck instantly raised and every instinct in her body told her to help the woman.

"Please, Henry!" the woman begged. "You're *hurting* me!"

The woman's pleas fell on deaf ears. He dragged her towards the stairs, her long jet-black hair flying over her face. Julia stood and watched, completely numb, but fully expecting the man to fling her down the stairs.

"Our marriage is *over*, Mary," he yelled, tossing the woman to the floor at the top of the stairs. "It's been over for a long time. I've had enough of you digging your claws into my fortune."

He hurried back into the room, and two more black bags flew over the balcony, landing with the others. Julia and Sue jumped back, both of them looking at the woman who was sobbing at the top of the stairs.

"Henry, let's talk about this," Mary pleaded, her accent distinctly English against Henry's. "I love you."

"You wouldn't know love if it hit you in the *face!*" he cried again, appearing at the top of the stairs with a suitcase in his hands. "You've got an hour to get out before I call the police."

He opened the case and projected the clothes into the air. Before they even had time to flutter to the ground, he launched the suitcase after it. It cracked and split into two halves on impact.

"*Dad!*" a voice called from behind the reception desk. "*Guests!*"

Henry glared down at Julia and Sue, before turning and disappearing back into the room, slamming the door behind him once more.

Julia turned to the young woman behind the counter, unsure of what to do. She looked to Sue, who shrugged as Mary's sobs echoed around the grand hall.

"Is she okay?" Julia asked, looking down at the woman's name badge, which read 'Charlotte McLaughlin'. "She seems quite upset."

"Leave her," Charlotte snapped, her tone cold. "She brought this on herself. Total gold-digger, just like the last three. I'm sorry you had to witness that, but it's been a long time coming."

"It's a good job we're not paying, or I'd ask for some discount!" Dot cried, her face red and eyes wide. "Quite *unacceptable*, young lady!"

"I can only apologise," Charlotte said through almost gritted teeth. "So, you must be the competition winners. Welcome to Seirbigh Castle. I hope you had a pleasant drive through our beautiful corner of the world."

Despite her friendly smile and soft Scottish accent, Julia could tell the girl was reading the lines from a mental script she had recited hundreds of times. She was strikingly beautiful, with large doe eyes and thick lashes, and soft auburn hair, which cascaded over her shoulders, only stopping in the small of her back. Faint freckles scattered her nose and cheeks, which only made her pale green eyes even more striking. Just like the beautiful landscape outside, it looked as though the woman had been painted by a skilled artist's brush.

"Let me show you to your rooms," Charlotte said as she pulled two keys off the board behind her. "I've got you down in one double and a twin room."

Before they could debate who got what, Dot snatched the double bed key out of Charlotte's hand

and smiled unapologetically at her granddaughters. Julia couldn't begrudge her gran the bigger bed; it was her competition prize after all.

Sue picked up the bags once more and headed awkwardly towards the foot of the stairs, stepping over the large pile of clothes and broken suitcase. Mary was still sobbing at the top.

"*This* way," Charlotte called over, stopping Sue before her foot even touched the bottom step. "That's staff quarters. Out of bounds to guests."

Sue frowned and turned on her heels before stepping back over the clothes. Julia scooped up the rest of the bags, grateful that Dot had at least grabbed one of the lighter ones this time. They followed Charlotte through a door, and along a narrow stone corridor, with windows on either side looking out onto the loch, which wasn't any less striking on second viewing. They entered one of the other parts of the castle, which appeared to be the largest and most recently built, although still centuries old.

"The spa and pool are through there," Charlotte said, directing a finger towards the end of the corridor as they walked to a less grand, but still stunning, sweeping staircase. "Breakfast is served at eight sharp every morning. You'll find the dining room by going back towards reception and through the double doors to the left of the office. Lunch and dinner are served at twelve and seven respectively. Since you're the only guests, try not to be late."

"*Only* guests?" Dot asked, a faint brow arching high.

"We've been quiet recently," Charlotte replied quickly, her customer service smile still plastered across her face, but something else entirely twinkling in her eyes. "Rest assured, you will still be getting the *best* treatment. We're running with a skeleton staff at the moment, but the spa is still fully functional."

"As it *should* be," Dot said with a stern nod.

They reached the top of the stairs and walked along another long corridor. Charlotte paused outside of one of the doors and took the key from Dot. She unlocked it and swung the door open. Julia felt her jaw drop before she realised she was doing it.

"Since we're empty, I thought I'd make use of our bridal suite," she said, glancing smugly to Dot. "I think you'll be quite comfortable in here."

Dot swallowed down a lump in her throat and nodded as she walked into the room. She walked straight over to the four-poster bed and looked to the large windows overlooking the loch. Julia knew it was a tactic as old as time, and one she had used herself in the café more than once. Always give the tricky customers something special because they're less likely to complain.

"I think I will," Dot said with a nod as she laid back on the bed and closed her eyes. "Put my things on the dresser, Julia."

Julia shuffled in and dropped her gran's bag, gazing at the beautifully decorated room, which looked bigger than her whole cottage combined. Elaborate tapestries covered the wood lined walls, with ornate mahogany furniture filling the space. Through an open door, Julia could see an ink-green tiled bathroom with a freestanding bath with gold feet. She would be happy if her bedroom were only half as beautiful as this one.

"You ladies are next door," Charlotte said, sounding eager to move them along. "There's an adjoining door if you would like me to unlock it?"

Sue glanced at their gran's room and shook her head. "It's okay. Keep it locked. I came here to relax."

Julia smirked as they carried their bags to the next door. She was relieved to see an equally beautiful smaller room, which was similarly decorated, with two wooden single beds next to each other.

"If you need anything, the phone on the bedside connects straight through to reception," Charlotte said as she bowed out of the room, her hand already on the door handle. "I hope you enjoy your stay."

"I'm sure we will," Sue said as she jumped onto the bed. "Thanks."

Unlike her gran's room, their room was on the corner of the building, so they had two windows. One was overlooking the loch, and the other looked over the rest of the castle. From this height, Julia could see her Ford Anglia parked in the shadows. Her eyes wandered to a figure sitting on the stumpy wall of the bridge with a pile of clothes at her feet. She realised it was Mary. She a packet of cigarettes from her pocket and with shaking hands, put one between her lips and lit it with a match.

"I wonder if she's going to be okay," Julia whispered.

"Who?" Sue mumbled through a content and calm smile. "The wife? Well, soon to be ex-wife. Who cares? It's not *our* problem. We're here to relax. Speaking of which, I think we should hit the spa *right now*."

Sue grabbed Julia's hand and dragged her towards the door. She looked back at her bed, wishing she could curl up and have a nap, but she

Shortbread and Sorrow

knew that wasn't why she had agreed to come on the trip. She had come for quality sister time, and even though face masks and massages were more Sue's style, she was sure she was going to enjoy every second of it with her little sister by her side.

CHAPTER 3

J ulia woke with a smile five minutes before her
alarm the next morning. Her skin felt soft with
the floral scent of the massage oil still lingering.
Her muscles felt relaxed and loose, and her mind was
clear and at peace. She looked over to Sue, who was
snoring soundly, a glistening trail of dribble across
her cheek. She snorted and rolled over, pulling the

covers over her head, as though she knew it was nearly time to wake up for breakfast.

After a quick shower in the freestanding bath, Julia quickly dressed in a simple dark grey knitted jumper, fitted black jeans, and trainers. She hadn't brought any of her typical 1940s style dresses with her because hadn't been sure the weather would call for it, but as she looked out of the window and down at the tranquil loch, she knew she had majorly misjudged the retreat.

Sue woke with her alarm, which had been set to go off at ten to eight. She groaned and rolled over, before sitting up in bed, her highlighted hair matted and sticking up. She looked around the room, her eyes landing on Julia in the dark, who was half hiding behind one of the curtains as she looked down at the loch.

"Morning, sleeping beauty," Julia exclaimed as she tossed back the heavy silk drapes. "Sleep well?"

Sue shielded her eyes and groaned even louder. Julia was sure she was about to try and go back to sleep, but she suddenly darted out of bed and hurried into the bathroom in her nightie. She slammed the door behind her and by the sounds of it, buried her head in the toilet.

"Are you okay in there?" Julia called through the

wood with a wince.

"Must have been the beef last night," she groaned back.

"I feel fine."

"You know I have a dodgy stomach."

Julia tried to remember if she knew that, but she couldn't recall that being a known fact about her sister. She remembered one time when they were kids that their friend, Roxy Carter, had pierced her own ear with a hot needle and a piece of apple, and Sue had thrown her guts up on the village green, but that was the only thing that sprung to mind.

Leaving her sister to get ready, Julia thought about calling Jessie or Barker to check how they were getting on. She got as far as hovering over the green call button, but hesitated, knowing they probably didn't need checking up on. She trusted them not to kill each other, or run her café into the ground.

She tossed her phone onto her bed and turned to look out of the other window and down at the rest of the castle. She immediately spotted Charlotte's striking auburn hair, which glistened brightly under the piercing morning sun. She was walking along the bridge where Mary had been sitting and crying with her clothes and cigarette the afternoon before. A tall redheaded man in a business suit was by her side. They appeared to laugh at something, not that Julia could hear it. She was sure if they looked up, they wouldn't see anything other than a shadow. When they reached the end of the bridge, they hugged and parted ways, with Charlotte walking up the slope towards the entrance, and the suited man disappearing around the side of the castle and out of view.

"What are you looking at?" Sue mumbled as she came out of the bathroom, wiping her mouth with the back of her hand and scratching her head with the other.

"Just taking in the view," Julia muttered as she watched Charlotte walk through the castle entrance. "We better get going. Gran won't miss a free breakfast for anything."

Just as Julia suspected, Dot was already waiting outside her room, obsessively checking her watch. With Sue trailing behind, they hurried down the staircase, along the corridor overlooking the loch, and into the entrance hall. Dot headed straight for the double doors by the reception desk, but Julia hung back to hold open the door for Sue, who had turned a ghostly shade of white.

"Why don't you go back to bed?" Julia suggested.

"I'll pass," Sue said with a shake of her head. "I'm already starting to feel better."

Julia smiled as supportively as she could, but her sister looked anything but '*better*', in fact, she looked worse than she had when she had stumbled out of the bathroom. When Sue walked through and headed towards the double doors, Julia let go of the door and turned to follow. A man had appeared at the reception desk, and for a moment, Julia wondered if he was the same man she had seen out on the bridge with Charlotte, but she immediately noticed he was much older. He was wearing a weighty brown overcoat, which had been patched up in many places. His sparse hair was wiry and coarse, sprouting out of the sides of his head without any style. He turned to Julia, a dark shadow of stubble covering the lower side of his face, and a definite smell of whisky on his breath.

"You my replacement?" he barked, his accent the thickest yet. "Cannae believe they've picked a lass to take over my job."

"Excuse me?"

"*You're* the new groundskeeper?"

"I'm a *guest*," Julia said with a small laugh. "But I'm sure if I *were* the new groundskeeper, I could do the job *just* as well as any man, thank you very much."

The man scowled and grunted. He shook his head and lumbered past her, the scent of moss and heather following him, hinting at a lifetime spent outdoors in the same jacket.

When the man vanished, Julia laughed in disbelief to herself and headed for the double doors. She walked down another corridor to a different part of the castle, and she came out into a long hallway lined with framed portraits. At the end, there was what looked like a glass sunroom overlooking the water. She guessed that was a more modern addition. An arrow on the wall pointed her to the dining hall, which was on the left through a wide stone arch opposite a room marked '*Drawing Room*'.

Dot and Sue were already sitting at a table in the middle of the empty dining room. There was a canteen style buffet, but the lights weren't turned on, and there was no food on display. Ceiling high windows looked out over the hills, flooding the room with light, but the cavernous room still looked dark and gloomy somehow.

"Sit down," Dot said, offering a chair to Julia. "Doesn't look like we're going to get served anytime soon. This place is run like a sinking ship!"

At that very moment, a flustered young woman

with rosy cheeks pushed through a door on the far side of the room. Her frizzy mousy hair flew free of the bun on top of her head, and her baggy apron was stained in flour and various sauces. It was a look Julia knew all too well.

"Sorry," she mumbled, her accent English, like Mary's. "I'm not used to serving. Orange juice and coffee?"

"*Tea*," Dot snapped, not seeming to notice the girl's stress. "And it better not be the *cheap* stuff!"

The girl dropped four tea bags into an already filled teapot, and placed it in the middle of the table with shaky hands. Julia attempted to give the young girl a smile, but it was either unwanted or unnoticed. Knowing how stressful a kitchen could be without the proper support, she hoped it was the latter. She could remember many times in her café's early days when she had been so overwhelmed that she had regretted ever opening.

The girl pulled out a notepad and scribbled down their breakfast orders. Dot ordered a full Scottish breakfast, making sure to mention the tattie scone and sautéed mushrooms specifically. The girl seemed relieved when Sue asked for corn flakes and Julia asked for poached eggs on toast. The sound of a full Scottish breakfast intrigued her, but she decided she would leave that for a day when she wasn't likely to cause the girl, who didn't look a day over nineteen, a breakdown.

"It's a good job we haven't paid for this," Dot whispered under her breath as the girl walked away. "Could you *imagine*?"

"Give her a break, Gran," Julia replied. "It's not easy doing it on your own. Charlotte said it was a skeleton staff at the moment, remember?"

"*Skeleton* staff?" Dot cried, craning her neck to look at the girl before she vanished back through the doors with her trolley. "She looks very much *alive* to me, sweetheart."

"It means they have the bare minimum working," Sue added, a little colour returning to her cheeks after a sip of tea. "It's what we do at the hospital during the late shifts and on days like Christmas."

"Well if this is the skeleton, I'd hate to see the ghost staff," Dot said through pursed lips. "Although, the lady in the spa is a miracle worker. I feel twenty-five again!"

To demonstrate, Dot cracked her neck and stretched out her arms. Julia laughed and glanced at the large windows, the view taking her breath away once more. She didn't care about the skeleton staff or the empty dining room, or even the ruckus that had welcomed them yesterday. Nothing could ruin the next five days of total relaxation.

There was a loud bang, and the doors opened again, making them all jump. The cook hurried back with their food, along with a rack of golden toast and a dish of yellow butter. When Julia smiled at her this time, she seemed to notice and smiled back, appearing relieved that breakfast was over for the morning.

"Thank you," Julia made an effort to say while their eyes briefly met.

"You're very welcome, miss," she said with a small nod before hurrying back through the doors again.

The doors banged again, causing Dot to slop baked beans down the front of her white blouse. She pursed her lips tightly and let out a long sigh through her flared nostrils as she dabbed at the stain with a napkin. Julia and Sue caught each other's eyes and shared a little grin.

Julia's eggs were poached to perfection, and Dot didn't complain once about her breakfast, which both sisters knew was a good sign. Sue barely touched her corn flakes, instead choosing to move them around the bowl while staring at them with a curled lip as though she was looking into a bowl of rotten eggs.

A third bang made them all jump, so much so that Julia spilt her tea in her lap. She dabbed up the tea with a napkin as she looked to the door, but the young cook didn't appear, and the doors were still in their frame.

"What was that?" Julia asked as she dried her jeans.

"Sounded like a gunshot," Sue whispered.

"Deer hunting is *very* popular around Loch Lomond," Dot exclaimed before reaching into her bag to pull out her guidebook. "Let me find the chapter. It's a fascinating read."

Julia glanced out of the window, but she couldn't see anybody on the bank ahead, despite the gunshot, if that's even what it was, sounding relatively close.

"I didn't know they had deer in Scotland," Sue said as she pushed her mushy cereal away. "I think the pool is calling this morning."

"That sounds like a good idea," Julia agreed as she screwed up the tea-soaked napkin and tossed it onto her plate. "Let's stack these up. Make the poor girl's job a little easier."

As Julia and Sue made the breakfast dishes as

neat as possible, Dot flicked through the pages of her tiny book, clicking her fingers together when she landed on the section about deer hunting.

"Ah, *here* it is!" she exclaimed, straightening her back before reading aloud. "*'Red deer hunting is a very popular sport in Scotland, particularly in the months of August and September'*."

"But it's only the end of May," Sue said.

Her gran opened her mouth to continue reading, but a piercing woman's scream echoed through the empty dining room. Dot turned to look at the doors to the kitchen, but Julia was sure it had come from the opposite direction.

"What was that?" Dot cried. "This place is a *shambles*! I'm going to be sure to call Tony Bridges and let him know -,"

"*Quiet, Gran*," Julia whispered, holding up her hand. "I can hear a woman crying."

Julia stood up and followed the sound through the dining room and back along the corridor that had taken her there in the first place. The sobbing grew louder and louder, pulling her back towards the entrance hall. Julia hurried along the corridor, and burst through the heavy doors with Sue and Dot hot on her heels.

Julia's hand drifted up to her mouth when she

saw Mary crouching over Henry, who was lying in a pool of blood and shattered pieces of wood. He was in the same place Mary's clothes had been the day before. Julia hurried forward and rested her hands on the woman's shoulders as she looked up at the landing. Just as she suspected, there was a huge chunk of the mahogany bannister missing where the man had fallen. Julia looked down at the man's body. When she noticed the blood pouring from his chest, she knew she had just discovered the source of the mysterious bang.

"He's been *shot*!" Mary wailed. "I was looking for him at the reception desk, and he just flew over and landed right here. *He's dead!*"

"Did you see who did it?" Julia whispered urgently. "Is there another way to get downstairs without being seen?"

"This is the only way," she sobbed. "*Oh, Henry!*"

At that moment, Charlotte appeared through the doors that led to the part of the castle where their sleeping quarters were. She walked in, her eyes instantly landing on her father. Instead of screaming out, she stared down at the body, before hurrying over to the reception desk to pick up the phone.

"*Police*," she said quickly down the handset as she held it to her face, her eyes wide as she continued to stare at her father. "Please, come quickly."

Julia left Mary's side and tiptoed up the sweeping staircase. She looked at the broken bannister, and then through the open door into what she assumed was Henry's bedroom. There was no murder weapon, and nobody else in sight. She took a step into the room and checked behind the door, making sure not to touch anything, but it was in vain; the room was empty.

Edging as close to the broken bannister as she dared, she stared down at Henry's body, wondering how the murderer had managed to flee without passing Mary. She had to stop herself from checking all of the other closed doors along the hall, deciding that was a job best left to the police. Knowing there was nothing else she could do yet, she pulled Mary away from her husband's body and comforted her at the bottom of the staircase.

While the grief-stricken woman sobbed against her shoulder, Julia pulled her in close and listened for the sirens.

CHAPTER 4

J ulia stared out of the window of the sunroom as the sun set on the loch. She attempted to focus on a man and child fishing in the distance, but the image of Henry's body was still fresh on her mind.

"How long are they going to keep us in here?" Dot moaned as she paced back and forth. "It's been *hours!*"

"They're going to interview everybody in the house," Julia explained calmly. "Including us."

"But we didn't *do* anything!"

"Then you'll have nothing to worry about," Sue added. "I don't see why they couldn't have made us stay in the spa or the pool room. It's an entire day of our trip wasted."

Julia looked sympathetically at her sister and smiled reassuringly, not sure how to tell her that the owner's murder was likely to put an end to their free trip. She decided it was better if she came to that conclusion on her own. She looked out at the water as pink and orange stained the horizon. It was beautiful, but it was a sunset she couldn't enjoy.

The shy young cook, who Julia had learned was called Blair, appeared in the doorway holding a fresh tray of tea and cakes. Julia gratefully took the tray from her, replacing the one she had brought in two hours ago.

"Do you know what's happening?" Dot asked, a little kinder than she had spoken to her earlier in the day. "I feel like they're not going to let us leave."

"I've just been interviewed," she said nervously, her fingers fumbling with the strings on her apron. "Told them I was in the kitchen the whole time. Men in white coats have been crawling all over the castle."

"Forensics," Julia mumbled, almost to herself. "Have they taken his body?"

"I think so, miss," Blair said with a quick nod.

"I've told you, it's *Julia*," she said with a kind smile. "Did you bake these? They look delicious."

"Lemon drizzle cupcakes, miss – *I mean* – Julia," she said, her voice soft and cheeks flushing at her own correction. "I've never seen a dead body before, but I walked past it when I took a tin of shortbread up to Charlotte. It's her favourite and I thought it might cheer her up. I think the poor woman is in shock. She hasn't said a word."

"Death can do that," Julia whispered, again to herself. "Although I did find it peculiar that she didn't call for an ambulance as well as the police. It was like she just assumed her father was already dead."

"Did you see the poor fella?" Dot mumbled through a mouthful of cake. "Oh, *Julia*! This girl might rival you. *Delicious*, Blair. Where was I? *Oh, yes*! The man was *clearly* dead. He had a huge chunk missing out of his -,"

Blair sniffled, and a flow of silent tears delicately streamed down her youthful cheeks. Julia wrapped a hand around her shoulders and pulled her into a little hug. It hadn't struck her that the girl had just lost her employer. From what Julia had seen of Henry, she hadn't very much liked the man herself, but she knew everybody had different sides to them.

"Why don't you sit down and enjoy your cakes?" Julia offered. "You've been rushed off your feet all day."

"No can do," Blair said quietly, quickly wiping her tears away as though they were forbidden. "I've got to clean the kitchen for Charlotte and Rory's dinner."

"Rory?" Julia asked.

"Charlotte's brother and Henry's – *his* son," she choked on the words before turning and hurrying off.

"Poor mite," Dot said as she plucked another cake from the tray. "She's a fragile one. She'll toughen up with age, but I can't imagine it's very pleasant seeing any man like that. *Oh*! This one has a *jam* filling!"

Dot tore open the cupcake and strawberry jam dribbled down her fingers. Dot licked it up and tossed the second cake into her mouth without a second thought. Julia was sure they were lovely, but her stomach wouldn't settle long enough to eat. She began to pace back and forth by the window as the light faded from the sky forcing the sconces to do their job. She was itching to know what was going on, and she desperately wanted to know what had happened.

"You've got *that* look in your eyes, Julia," Sue said sternly with a shake of her head. "I don't like *that* look."

"What look?"

"The look you get right before you wade into something," Dot replied for her. "It's like when a bull sees red."

"It's the waving of the flag that entices the bull, not the colour," Julia corrected her as she continued to pace. "Bulls are actually colour-blind. It could be a green flag or a red flag, and the bull would still charge."

"Well, murder is *your* flag," Dot said as she poured herself a cup of tea. "And this castle is waving it in front of you!"

Julia wanted to deny it, but her gran was right. She had been trying to piece things together ever since the police officers had chaperoned them into the sunroom and told them not to leave. Who had hated Henry so much that they would want to shoot him? Where did they get the gun? Why now?

"*Evening*, ladies."

Julia stopped in her tracks and turned to see a fresh-faced young man standing in the doorway. He had sandy blonde hair, which was slicked back off his smooth and shiny forehead. His overpowering sweet aftershave filled the room, turning Julia's stomach further. Just from his demeanour and suit, she knew he was with the police.

"Detective Inspector Fletcher," the man said as he flashed a badge, his Scottish accent soft and barely noticeable. "Jay Fletcher. May I have a seat?"

Julia motioned to the seat she had been sitting in earlier. She crossed her arms tightly over her chest and stared down at the man, waiting for some grand revelation. Instead, he frowned down at the cakes, and then up at Dot, who was grinning like a Cheshire cat as she bit into another cake. Jam dribbled down her chin and onto her already stained blouse.

"I know you ladies were together in the dining room when Henry McLaughlin died so this won't take long," he said as he pulled a pad from his jacket pocket. "I just want to know your account of things, in your own words."

"Aren't you a little young to be a DI?" Dot said. "You're fresh out of Pampers."

The handsome young man smirked and shook

his head. It was clear it wasn't the first time he had heard that. Julia wouldn't have guessed the man had even passed his thirtieth birthday yet.

"I assure you, I'm more than competent," he said sternly, his charismatic smile still plastered across his face. "Who wants to go first?"

"We were eating breakfast in the dining room alone," Julia started, taking a step forward. "Blair, the cook, was coming in and out, serving us. We heard the gunshot, and we thought it might be deer hunters, but we realised it was out of season. Then, I heard Mary scream and I followed the sound of her crying to the entrance hall. We stayed by her side until the police arrived. Do you know who murdered Henry?"

"It's my job to ask the questions," he said with a small laugh. "I didn't catch your name."

"Julia South," she said quickly. "This is my gran, Dot, and my sister, Sue. But it was murder, right? He was shot in the chest. I can't see that being an accident."

"We're not ruling anything out."

"A wound like that must have been from a pretty powerful gun," Julia said, her eyes glazing over as she stared down at the cakes in the dim light. "It didn't sound like a handgun. There was too much echo. Too much of a bang. Besides, if deer hunting is popular here, you would expect people to have rifles of some kind. Unless you have very long arms, it's almost impossible to shoot yourself in the chest with a rifle, unless you cut the end off, but don't most people go for the head if they want to end their own life? No point prolonging it, and doing it so publically where you can possibly fall and break through a bannister."

Julia met the DI's eyes, and he stared at her, a mixture of disbelief and suspicion filling his young face. She suddenly remembered she wasn't in Peridale anymore, and this wasn't Barker.

"You seem to know a lot, Miss South."

"She's an *astute* woman," Dot exclaimed proudly. "Assisted on many murder cases back home."

"And where is home?" he asked, his pen hovering over his paper.

"Peridale," Sue said. "The Cotswolds. Beautiful little village."

"*Peridale?*" he echoed, tapping the pen on his chin. "Sounds familiar. Think I heard about a DI down there who was suspended for letting some baker run his murder investigation. Funny how quickly those kinds of silly things get around.

Wouldn't know anything about that, would you Julia?"

"No," she lied.

"We all had a good laugh about that up here," he said, shaking his head with a smirk. "Wouldn't get that happening up in Scotland, I'll tell you that."

Julia's cheeks burned brightly, and she looked down at the floor, avoiding his eyes. She turned and stared through the windows, but the sun had completely fallen out of the sky, so all she could see was her own reflection looking back at her in the glass. Behind her, she noticed the DI standing up, taking one of the cakes as he did.

"Since you're checked in until Monday morning, I'd like you to stick around," he said as he peeled the wrapper off the small cake. "I'm satisfied that you've told me all you know, for now, but I can't have you leaving the country, can I?"

"They're keeping the spa open?" Julia asked, quickly turning around.

"Charlotte thinks it is for the best," he replied. "We can only advise. They have *paying* guests checking in before the weekend, and they can't afford to lose the business. Call me if you think of anything else, ladies."

He passed Julia a business card, popped the cake

into his mouth, looked each of them in the eyes, and then turned and sauntered slowly down the hallway and through the double doors at the end.

"He doesn't know a thing," Julia said quickly as she turned the card over in her hands before pocketing it. "If he suspects the three women with concrete alibis, he's grasping at straws."

"You shouldn't have let him know so much," Sue said, her eyes strained with concern. "You made it sound like you were involved, or even guilty."

"I was just piecing together the obvious," Julia said, shrugging dismissively and turning back to the window. "I didn't tell him anything he shouldn't have already figured out hours ago."

"Do we have to stay here all night?" Dot asked as she unpeeled her fourth cupcake.

"I would expect we were the last on his list of suspects to interview," Julia said, already heading for the door. "After this amount of time, I'd say forensics are likely to have everything they need."

Dot stuffed her handbag with the rest of the cakes, sipped the last of the tea, and hurried through the door and down the corridor. Sue was more hesitant, not taking her eyes away from Julia as she walked towards her.

"You're up to something," Sue whispered when

they were face to face. "I know you."

"I'll follow you up in ten minutes," Julia said, nodding for her to follow their gran. "I want to offer my services to Blair. If we're here for the next five days, I don't want to sit around getting pampered now that a man has died."

Sue nodded that she understood, but Julia could see the disappointment flickering in her eyes. Julia gave her a quick kiss on the cheek and a hug.

"We'll still have sister time," Julia reassured her.

Sue smiled and dropped her head before hurrying along the corridor towards the double doors, where Dot was waiting for her. Julia smiled and waited until they had left, before turning to the dark dining room and darting in between the tables towards the door at the end of the room.

Without hesitation, she pushed through the doors and into another dark room. When her eyes adjusted, she noticed a large dumbwaiter elevator, which told her the kitchen was in the basement. She spotted a narrow stone staircase, and hurried towards it, not wanting to waste a second.

The steps were steep and cold, and they wound in a spiral, leading her deep into the island. When she reached the bottom, she pushed on a small door, fluorescent lights instantly blinding her.

Blair was by the sink, washing the dishes while the radio played pop music next to her. Julia looked around the kitchen, surprised by how modern it was. Some serious money had gone into the equipment, and it made her a little jealous that her café's kitchen wasn't anywhere near as well stocked. She took a couple of steps forward before clearing her throat.

It wasn't her intention to startle Blair, but she understood why she did. The girl spun around, and a white plate slid from her pink rubber gloved hands and shattered against the exposed stone floor.

"*Sorry,*" Julia said, hurrying over and picking up the biggest shards of porcelain. "I didn't mean to scare you."

"It's okay," Blair said with a small laugh as she rested her hand on her chest. "I'm just not used to people coming down here. It's been pretty quiet 'round here recently."

Julia spotted a dustpan and brush next to a mop bucket in the corner, so she swept up the mess she had caused so Blair could carry on with her job. The girl smiled gratefully down at her.

"Your accent doesn't fit in here," Julia said as she tossed the shards into the bin. "English?"

"Blackpool," she said with a nod. "Moved up here for this job. There wasn't much going on back home, and I couldn't resist the idea of working in a spa."

"Have you baked long?"

"My whole life," she said, her cheeks flushing. "It's the only thing I'm good at. My mum taught me."

"Mine too," Julia said. "She died when I was a little girl, but she passed on a lot of her knowledge."

"Oh, I'm sorry," Blair whispered, dropping her face. "You bake?"

"I own a café."

"A *café?*" Blair remarked, smiling shyly through her stray strands of hair. "That's my dream."

Julia returned the girl's smile. She had sensed they were similar, but she hadn't realised how much they really had in common.

"That's part of the reason I came down here," Julia said, stepping forward and leaning against the counter. "To offer my services."

"Services?"

"Free of charge, of course," Julia said with a curt nod. "DI Jobs-Worth up there wants me to stick around until Monday, and I'm not really one for spas and pampering. I feel most comfortable in a kitchen, and I'm itching to get stuck into some baking. You seemed pretty rushed off your feet this morning."

"Oh, that's very kind of you," Blair said, shaking her head as she focussed on the dishes. "But, I don't think Charlotte will like that."

"Does she ever come down here?"

"Well, *no*, but -,"

"Then nobody has to know," Julia urged, nudging her with her shoulder. "I'll even share my secret recipes with you, and I'll tell you all about how I opened my own café."

The offer of knowledge from a more experienced baker made Blair's eyes light up, just as Julia had hoped. Her heart pounded in her chest, and she almost felt guilty for using it as a bribe against the girl, but she knew it was the only way she was going to have access to the people and information she needed.

"Until Monday?" Blair asked, her eyes squinting.

"And then I'll be gone."

Blair appeared to think about it for a moment before nodding and facing Julia with a soft smile.

"It would be nice to bake with somebody for once," Blair admitted.

"Then it's settled," Julia said, holding out a hand for Blair to shake. "I'll be here bright and early in the morning."

Shortbread and Sorrow

Blair reached out to shake her hand with the pink rubber glove, but stopped herself and ripped it off before accepting Julia's hand. Her skin was soft, and her grip was weak. She reminded Julia so much of her younger self. She could almost sense the same fear of the future that had consumed Julia at that age.

"It will be fun," Blair said, a smile taking over soft features.

"It will be," Julia agreed, before feigning a yawn. "I should follow my sister up to bed for now. It's been a long day."

Julia rested a hand softly on Blair's shoulder, and she nodded her understanding. Leaving her to finish the washing up, Julia walked swiftly towards the door and back up the spiralling staircase, knowing she had just discovered her key to unlocking the secrets that Seirbigh castle held.

CHAPTER 5

Julia woke with the sunrise and was showered, dressed, and out of the bedroom before Sue had even had a chance to stir. She had spent most of the previous evening trying to convince Julia to stay out of things and take advantage of the treatments on offer, but Julia would rather put her mind to good use instead of pretending to be a piece of sushi in a seaweed wrap.

Shortbread and Sorrow

As she walked along the stone corridor joining the bedrooms and the entrance hall, she paused and looked out over the loch. The sky was still pale and grey, and the water completely still. She closed her eyes and inhaled the crisp morning air. There wasn't a sound for miles. It reminded her of the early mornings in Peridale when she could sit in her garden and enjoy the quiet of the countryside before the village woke and started their daily gossiping.

She reluctantly tore herself away from the view and walked through to the entrance hall. She hadn't been expecting to see anybody, so she stopped in her tracks and jumped a little when she saw Mary standing behind the desk in a navy blue pantsuit, her black hair scraped back into a neat ponytail, and a professional smile on her red-stained lips.

"Somebody is up early," she remarked, smiling effortlessly at Julia. "Off for a quiet dip before the others rise?"

Julia looked down at the floor to where the woman's husband had been lying dead less than twenty-four hours ago. She craned her neck to get a good look at the bannister, which had been patched up with bright yellow caution tape, and then back at Mary. Julia attempted to return the smile, but her bafflement restrained her cheeks from moving more than a couple of millimetres.

"I'm actually going down to the kitchen to give Blair a helping hand with breakfast," Julia said, casting a finger absently towards the double doors. "I run a café, so I thought I would make myself useful."

"That's very kind of you but quite unnecessary," Mary said, her smile unwavering. "You're a *guest* here, and Blair can more than cope."

"I honestly don't mind," Julia insisted, forcing her smile a little wider. "I like keeping my hands busy."

"Well, in that case, I'm sure she'll appreciate the help."

Julia nodded her agreement and hurried towards the doors. She didn't realise she had stopped breathing until she was on the other side of the double doors. As she rushed through the silent and shadowy dining room, she couldn't believe she had just come face to face with the same sobbing woman she had held at the foot of the stairs only the day before.

"Morning," Julia said, pushing Mary to the back of her mind as she walked into the kitchen. "Something smells good."

"I'm making Charlotte and Rory's breakfast," Blair said. "Charlotte is an early riser, so I thought I would try and keep things as normal as I could for her."

"Does Rory live here too?" Julia asked as she took one of the frying pans Blair was trying to juggle. "I don't think I've met him."

"He lives in Aberfoyle. He's a lawyer," Blair said as she flipped the bacon. "He's here a lot. They usually don't tell me when he's here for meals, so I have to go out and look to see if his car is there."

"And what about Mary?" Julia asked, unable to shake the woman from her mind. "What's her role here?"

"She's the manager," Blair said as she flipped the bacon once more. "Can you put some toast under the grill? The bread is in that bin there."

Julia nodded and assisted the girl as she wished. She was so used to being the one juggling the pans and the dishes that it was surprisingly enjoyable to take the backseat role and carry out the orders.

"I'm surprised she's here," Julia said. "When I arrived yesterday, Henry was throwing her out."

"That happens a lot," Blair said, glancing awkwardly at Julia out of the corner of her eyes. "She's his *fourth* wife, but from what I've heard, she's the one who has stuck around for the longest, aside from the first one."

"How long?"

"Three years."

"So not very long at all," Julia whispered under her breath. "And the first wife? I guess that is Charlotte and Rory's mother?"

"Henry's one true love, or so they *say*. Sandra died during childbirth when Charlotte was born. People say Charlotte is like her mother's twin."

"And what was Charlotte's relationship like with her father?"

Blair gave Julia a curious look as she spun around and started serving up the breakfasts. Julia busied herself with cutting the toast into triangles and slotting them neatly into the silver toast rack. She decided it was better to wait for Blair to speak voluntarily instead of bombarding her with more questions.

"It is – *I mean* – it *was* frosty," Blair whispered, glancing over to the door as though Charlotte was going to burst through at any moment. "Charlotte's *official* role is customer services. She deals with bookings and checking in the guests, but everybody knows she wants to manage this place. She resents working under her stepmother. The story goes that anyone who marries Henry becomes the manager."

"Is Mary a good manager?"

Shortbread and Sorrow

Blair blushed and dropped her face a little as she poured the baked beans onto the plates. Her silence spoke more than a thousand words.

"She's inexperienced," Blair said tactfully. "She thinks I'm enough to cook and serve during the quiet times, but we've got two couples checking in for the weekend, and she still thinks I'm going to be able to do it all on my own. There was another girl here, but she was fired a week after I arrived two months ago. I was thinking about it last night, and I'm so grateful that you're here because I was worried about juggling everything. On top of that, the McLaughlin's use me as their personal chef. Rory is the worst for it, and he doesn't even work here. He'll call down when I'm in the middle of preparing dinner and tell me he's bringing five friends 'round for a hot tub party and he'll order the most complicated things. A lot of the time, I don't even have the food here, so I have to send somebody into the village."

"He sounds lovely," Julia joked with a wink.

"Between you and me, he gives me the creeps," Blair whispered back. "Can you grab the jug of orange juice from the fridge? I squeezed it fresh an hour ago, so it should be cold enough now. I'll make up a pot of tea, and then I'm ready to serve."

Julia fetched the jug while Blair prepared the tea. She looked down at the trolley, but couldn't figure out where to put the jug with the plates, toast, butter dish, and cutlery. When Blair returned, she was pushing a separate trolley with the teapot, two cups and saucers, a dish with sugar cubes, and a jug of milk. Julia set the jug onto that trolley and grabbed two small glasses from the display on the wall. Blair smiled, plucked up the glasses and replaced them with two different ones. Julia chuckled apologetically.

"And you manage this on your own?"

"I have the dumbwaiter," Blair said, hooking her thumb over her shoulder to the elevator next to the door. "I have to carry the trolleys one by one up the stairs though."

"On your own?"

"I make two trips."

"I'll help you," Julia offered, closing her hands around the food trolley as Blair set two domed silver cloches over the plates. "It's far too much to carry on your own."

"You should stay down here."

Julia hurried over to the wall and plucked an apron off one of the coat hooks. She took her hair out of the ponytail and crafted her curls into a bun that matched Blair's.

"If they say anything, I'll take the blame," Julia said as she pushed the trolley into the dumbwaiter. "Besides, they've got more important things to worry about today."

Blair reluctantly pushed the second trolley into the dumbwaiter, closed it and pressed some buttons on the panel. The lift shuddered into life and sent the food up to the next floor.

"You can wait outside the bedroom," Blair whispered as she held the door open for Julia, a mischievous smile taking over her usually shy expression.

They met the trolleys on the next floor and pushed them quickly through the dining room and back towards the entrance hall. Blair seemed grateful to have Julia if only to hold the doors open for her. They whizzed past the reception desk, where Mary was talking on the phone. Julia noticed a young man in a green Barbour jacket she hadn't seen before crouching over the fireplace and stacking up logs of freshly chopped wood to start a fire. He glanced over his shoulder when he heard the rattling trolleys and smiled at Blair. She smiled back, blushing a little, before picking up the trolley and hurrying up the stairs. Before Julia had time to think of the best way to do it, she hoisted up the trolley under her arms and hurried up the stairs, hoping gravity and her thirty-seven-year-old knees would spare her the embarrassment this time. When she reached the top step, she let out a relieved sigh.

"It looks so much higher from up here," Julia panted as she cast her attention to the broken bannister.

Blair nodded, but she didn't say anything. She couldn't bring herself to look at the wood. Julia couldn't blame the girl. She was almost glad the family were keeping Blair so busy, so she didn't have to linger and think about what had actually happened here. Julia, on the other hand, could think of nothing else.

"*Oh no!*" Blair exclaimed, stopping in her tracks. "I've forgotten the ketchup. Rory insists on smothering everything in the stuff. He's like a child."

"I can go back," Julia offered, looking back down the stairs.

"It's easier if I do," Blair said, already hurrying past Julia. "I'll be quicker, and I know where it is. Just wait here and don't go inside."

Julia nodded her promise that she wouldn't. She looked to the door that Blair had been heading towards and waited until the girl was hurrying back through the double doors and towards the kitchen. She pushed the trolleys towards the door, which was slightly ajar. A picture on the wall caught her eye. It depicted a man, who she instantly recognised as Henry McLaughlin, with a small boy and girl a couple of steps in front of him. They were standing tall on the bridge in front of the castle, with their chins pushed forward with smile-less expressions. It wasn't the type of family picture that Julia would have hung on display. In the shadows of the castle walls, she pushed her hands into her apron and bowed her head, all while tilting her ear towards the gap.

"They *know* it was Father's gun from the mantelpiece in the drawing room," she heard a man say. "You *know* he kept that thing loaded."

"*Everyone* knew it," she heard Charlotte whisper back. "He did it to scare people. Just relax."

"Jokes on him now," the man returned with a soft laugh. "You didn't tell the police I was here yesterday, did you?"

"Of course not!" she replied. "Can you imagine how that would look?"

Silence fell, and Julia held her breath, sure she was about to be caught in the act of eavesdropping.

When she saw Blair scuttling back towards her holding a bottle of ketchup, red-faced and breaking out in a sweat, she let out a relieved sigh.

"Wait here," Blair instructed as she backed up and pushed herself against the door with the trolleys trailing behind.

Blair entered the room, and Julia did as she was told. She hung back, but she took her opportunity to look inside. She caught a glimpse of Charlotte sitting up in bed in a silk robe, with a similarly redheaded man in a business suit lying across the bottom of her bed while reading a broadsheet. Neither of them looked particularly grief-stricken or heartbroken that their father had been murdered just down the hall the day before. Before the door slammed shut, the man turned to look at her, but when he saw her apron, he looked back at his newspaper. Julia couldn't be certain, but she was fairly sure he was the same redheaded man she had seen Charlotte talking with and hugging on the bridge the morning of Henry's murder.

Julia was broken from her train of thought when she heard the unmistakable sound of two plates, two full Scottish breakfasts, and two domed metal cloches clattering against the wooden floor. Despite her strict instructions to stay outside, Julia was bursting through the door and hurrying over to help before she even realised what she was doing.

"You *stupid* girl!" Charlotte cried furiously, sitting up sternly in bed. "Are you *trying* to get yourself *fired?*"

Blair shook her head, tears already rolling down her face. Julia dipped down and dropped her head away from Charlotte as she helped Blair gather up the mess into the two metal cloches.

"S-s-sorry, miss," Blair stuttered. "I'll make you fresh ones right away, *m-m-miss*."

"As you should," Rory, the brother, exclaimed, nodding firmly at both of them. "I tell you, sis, you can't get the staff these days."

Blair and Julia cleaned up as much of the mess as they could before putting it on one of the trolleys and hurrying out of the room. The second they were outside, Blair broke down and fell into Julia's arms.

"I'm sorry, Julia," she stumbled through her tears. "I just can't shake the image of Henry's body from my mind. It haunted my dreams all night."

"I understand," Julia whispered as she stroked the back of the girl's hair. "I've been there myself more times than I would like to admit."

"You've seen dead bodies?"

"My fair share."

"Does it get easier?"

"Sure it does," Julia said, hoping the shake in her voice didn't reveal the lie. "Let's go down to the kitchen and make you a nice cup of hot tea. Have you ever tried peppermint and liquorice? I have a couple of teabags in my room."

* * *

JULIA INHALED HER FAVOURITE TEA, AND she instantly felt at home. She thought about Mowgli, Jessie, and Barker, and suddenly she found herself missing Peridale. She turned to Blair as she took her first sip, and was pleased when she didn't recoil in horror.

"It's delicious," Blair said as she wiped the tears from her cheeks. "Do you serve this in your café?"

"It's on the menu, although I think I'm the only person who drinks it."

"Do you have a lot of cakes on your menu?"

"The majority is cakes," Julia said with a small chuckle. "Sometimes I think I'm the only person in the village people trust to bake them anything. It's a burden I enjoy."

"And you do it all alone?"

"I have Jessie," Julia said before taking another

deep sip of the hot tea. "I took her in off the streets. She was homeless, but now she's my apprentice and my lodger. She's not much younger than you."

"You must be a kind woman," Blair said, her smile soft, but noticeably sad. "She's a lucky girl."

The door to the kitchen squeaked open, but Blair didn't act as startled as she had when Julia had crept in, nor did she look surprised to see the handsome man who had been lighting the fire in the entrance hall. The lower half of his face was taken up with a short beard, but his line-free eyes and low hairline told Julia the man wasn't much older than Blair.

"I thought I heard you crying," he said as he hurried over, the scent of heather and moss lingering on his green overcoat. "Are you alright?"

"I dropped Charlotte and Rory's breakfasts," Blair said with a stifled laugh. "Right in front of them."

"Oh, sis," the man said as he wrapped his arm around her shoulders. "Mam always said you were born with two left hands and two right feet."

The young man looked at Julia and smiled kindly at her as he comforted his sister. Julia was relieved to learn that Blair wasn't alone in the large castle, especially considering what had happened.

"This is my brother, Benjamin," Blair said. "Ben, this is Julia. She's a guest, but she's helping me out. She owns a café."

"A café?" Benjamin exclaimed as he reached out to awkwardly shake Julia's hand with his left arm, catching her off guard and forcing her to quickly switch hands. "That's my sister's dream, isn't it Blair? It's nice to meet you."

"You too," Julia said as she let go of the young man's hand. "Did you move up here together?"

"I came up first," Blair said. "When Henry fired Andrew McCracken, I put in a good word for Ben."

"There aren't many jobs back home," Benjamin explained. "Not since the recession. Tourism isn't what it was, and I didn't fancy working behind a bar. I've always been an outdoors kind of guy, so the groundskeeper job suited me perfectly."

"So *you're* the new groundskeeper," Julia said with a nod. "I think somebody mistook me for you yesterday. There was a man at reception who asked if I was the new groundskeeper. Quite rude, actually."

Benjamin took a sharp intake of breath and pushed his hands behind his coat to rest them on his slender hips. He nodded his understanding and rolled his eyes a little, reminding Julia of Jessie.

"I guess you've met Andrew," he said. "I only

arrived a few weeks ago, but he's been up here quite a lot. Probably trying to get his job back. I've avoided meeting the fella so far, but I can't see it happening much longer."

"He's a drunk," Blair explained with a whisper. "Not a very nice man."

Julia opened her mouth to speak, but she suddenly stopped herself. She realised that she had seen Andrew on the morning Henry was murdered, meaning he was in the castle right before it had happened. The cogs in her mind started to crank slowly as the pieces slotted into place.

"Does Andrew live quite close?" Julia asked.

"Last I heard, he was staying above a pub in Aberfoyle," Blair said.

"Do you know which pub?"

"Is it significant?"

Julia thought for a moment, smiling as not to give away her genuine motives.

"I wanted to go into the village with my sister, and I wondered if it was a good pub," she said, hoping the first thing that sprung to her mind was good enough.

It appeared to be. Neither sibling looked too suspiciously at her.

"The Red Deer Inn," Blair said. "Although it's

not the nicest place to eat. You might be better trying one of the little tearooms or cafés on the backstreets. We should get on with remaking Charlotte and Rory's breakfasts before we need to start on your gran and sister's."

While Blair gathered the ingredients from the fridge, Julia pulled her notepad out of her handbag, flicked past a recipe for a double chocolate fudge cake, and scribbled down '*Andrew McCracken - The Red Deer Inn*'. If the former groundskeeper who had been fired by the victim only two weeks previously was lurking around the castle on the morning of Henry's murder, Julia wanted to speak to him.

CHAPTER 6

J ust after lunch, Julia and Sue drove into Aberfoyle village, leaving their gran to enjoy the spa. Julia had intentionally waited until the masseuse had carefully placed the cucumber slices on Dot's eyes before grabbing Sue and dragging her out of the castle.

"You've got flour in your hair," Sue said as they drove slowly through the village as the afternoon sun beat down on them. "Why do you think this man will be able to tell you something, anyway?"

"Because he was there the morning Henry was murdered," Julia said as she tried to look around the car in front to see what was causing the holdup. "Even if he can't tell us anything about that morning, he might be able to paint a picture of Henry so I can try and figure out who would want to murder him."

"Well, there's only so many people it could be," Sue said with a sigh. "I was thinking about this while Maria was giving me a deep tissue massage. Aside from us, the only people in the castle when Henry was shot were Charlotte and Blair, so it must have been one of those two."

"Blair was down in the kitchen, and from what I can see, there was only one door out of that room, and it led to the dining room. We would have seen her."

"Don't these old castles have secret tunnels?"

Julia almost laughed off the suggestion, until she realised it wasn't entirely ridiculous. If Charlotte had been the one to shoot her father with the gun she had known was sitting loaded in the drawing room, it would explain how she had come to be on the other side of the castle right before she had seen him.

Shortbread and Sorrow

Julia still hadn't been able to shake the cold and distant look in Charlotte's eyes when she had seen her father's corpse.

"I suppose," Julia agreed with a nod as they turned down a small cobbled backstreet. "But they weren't the only two in the castle, were they? Mary was there too. She found his body."

"But she couldn't have done it," Sue said with a small laugh of disbelief. "Those tears were *real*."

"Or very well acted," Julia mumbled. "You should have seen her this morning, Sue. She was behind the reception desk in a pantsuit ready for a day of work like nothing had happened. She didn't look like a woman who had just lost her husband."

"Let's not forget the man had thrown her out the day before," Sue added. "I wonder why she came back when she found his body."

"Maybe to reason with him?"

"Probably."

"Or maybe to kill him?"

"*Or* that," Sue said with a roll of her eyes. "Although I don't believe she did. Either way, she's a lucky woman. She died the man's wife, so I guess that means she keeps his fortune. Another couple of months and a divorce later, and she wouldn't have been entitled to a penny."

"You sound just like Gran."

"Well, it's true," Sue whispered. "You have to think about these things. Maybe she was chipper this morning because she realised she had landed on her feet. A castle like that would be worth more than a few quid."

"From what I heard from Blair, Charlotte isn't going to stand by and let her stepmother take over the running of the castle. Blair thinks Mary only got the job as manager because she was married to the king of the castle."

"It would explain why the place was so quiet," Sue said with another heavy sigh. "It's a beautiful spa, but it would be nicer if there were more guests to talk to. In fact, it would be nice if I had my *sister* by my side to relax with me. Gran is already driving me up the wall!"

Julia smiled apologetically to her sister as she pulled into the car park in front of The Red Deer Inn. She looked up at it, and it lacked all of the charms of The Plough pub in the heart of Peridale. It was a nondescript building that Julia wouldn't have even recognised as a pub if it weren't for the giant red sign and the lopsided parasols jutting out of the plastic tables cluttering the entrance.

"He couldn't have lived above a quaint

tearoom?" Sue groaned as she got out of the car. "Or a nice little jewellery shop?"

The two sisters linked arms as they walked towards the pub. Burly men in white vests exposing their bulked-up and tattoo covered arms glanced at the two women. Julia stiffened her back a little and tried her best not to make eye contact with the men, who she was sure were trying everything to do just that.

"It stinks of beer," Sue said with a gag as they stepped into the dark and musty pub. "I'm so glad my Neil isn't a drinker. It's making me feel sick."

Julia couldn't disagree with her sister. As they walked towards the bar, she tried her best to take short intakes of breath through her mouth. The dank pub stank of stale cigarette smoke worked into the wood decades before the smoking ban, spilt stale ale soaked into the carpets, and greasy peanuts, which were scattered across the cluttered bar.

An old man looked from under his hat at the two women, groaned and returned to his pint. Sue clung even tighter onto Julia's arm.

"I think we should order a drink," Julia whispered. "To blend in."

"I'll have an orange juice," Sue replied. "And make sure to ask for a *clean* glass."

Julia nodded and decided an orange juice was a good idea, especially since they had to drive back down the winding lanes to the castle. She leant over the bar and caught the attention of the only other woman she had seen since entering.

"You lost?" the woman barked in her thick Scottish accent, her tone clearly condescending. "We dinnae do afternoon tea."

The woman was a few years older than Julia, but she looked like she had lived a harder life. Her wiry peroxide blonde hair was scraped up into a loosely pinned roll at the back of her head. A large black beauty spot balanced on her top lip, which bounced up and down as she spoke. Her leopard print blouse left little to the imagination.

"Two orange juices please," Julia said, trying her best to smile, not that she thought it was going to help.

"English too?" the woman scoffed, shaking her head as she collected two glasses from above her. "Dinnae get your kind 'round these parts too often. Sure yer nae lost, lassie?"

"We're actually looking for somebody," Julia said as she swallowed hard and smiled even wider. "A Mr McCracken? We heard he rents a room here?"

"What's it to you?" she snapped.

Julia took her lack of denial as confirmation that she was at least in the right place. She wriggled her arm free of Sue's and pulled her purse from her small bag. She pulled out a Scottish ten-pound note that she had changed at the post office before leaving Peridale, and pushed it across the bar.

"Keep the change," Julia said. "We just wanted to ask him some questions. A man has been murdered at Seirbigh Castle, and we thought he ought to know."

"Are you the polis?"

"Do you mean '*police*'?" Sue asked, arching a brow and glancing at Julia.

"*That's* what I *said*," the woman replied flatly as she poured orange juice from a carton and into the two glasses. "*Polis.*"

"No," Julia answered, giving her sister a look that she hoped read as '*leave the talking to me*'. "We're just friends. We just wanted to let him know since it was his former employer."

"Henry McLaughlin, yer say?" she asked, suddenly frowning as she picked up the money from the bar. "He's been morrdered?"

"*Huh?*" Sue jumped in.

"Done in," the woman barked, glaring at Sue.

"Killed. *Murdered*."

"Yes, he's been murdered," Julia said quickly before her sister could speak again. "Mr McCracken?"

The barmaid looked down at the drinks, then to the money in her hand, then to Julia, and then more disdainfully to Sue. She nodded silently into the corner of the room before turning her back on them and putting the money in the till. With her orange juice in hand, Julia turned and saw the man she had seen in the reception area on the morning of Henry's murder. She suddenly felt foolish for not scoping out the place first before asking the unfriendly locals.

Andrew McCraken was staring into a dark pint of bitter ale, still in his musty overcoat. The grey stubble on his face had grown even longer, and his thin hair looked even more out of place. He was sitting beneath a dreary oil painting of what appeared to be Loch Lomond with Seirbigh Castle in the distance. It didn't do the true beauty any justice. Julia and Sue walked over to his table, but he didn't look up.

"Excuse me? Andrew?" Julia asked politely. "You might not remember me, but we met two days ago at the castle?"

The man grunted and frowned, looking up from

his pint as though Julia had just interrupted a deep and important thought that he hadn't been able to keep hold of.

"*What?*" he slurred. "Can't a man enjoy his pint in *peace* anymore?"

Sue gave Julia a look that screamed '*please make this quick because I'm scared and I want to leave*', but Julia dismissed it and sat uninvited across the table from Andrew. She knew she wouldn't find out what she wanted to know if she was shy about it. Sue decided to stay hovering, like an unsure bumblebee buzzing over a dandelion.

"We met at the castle two days ago," Julia repeated, looking under Andrew's low and furrowed brow and into his eyes. "Do you remember me?"

The man shrugged and picked up his pint. He glugged half of it down, slammed it onto the table, and smeared his mouth with the sleeve of his jacket. From the brown stains cluttering his sleeve, this seemed like normal behaviour.

"If *she's* sent you down here to try and convince me, you can get away wi' yer," he barked, pointing a long and dirty fingernail in Julia's face. "A've had it with that place."

"Nobody sent us," Julia said, glancing up to Sue who looked just as confused. "I've come to ask you why you were at the castle on the morning Henry McLaughlin was shot down and murdered in his own home."

The man met her eyes, a flicker of anger crinkling them at the sides. He didn't seem surprised to hear that Henry was dead, which made Julia suspect he already knew. She wasn't sure if Aberfoyle was anything like Peridale, but news as exciting as a murder didn't stay quiet for long, even if the barmaid hadn't found out yet.

"Charlotte called me up there asking me to take my old job back," Henry mumbled, staring into the depths of his pint. "But I told her what I told her today! The man sacked me for being a drunk! *I'm no drunk*! I just like a drink. There's a difference *y'know*!"

"Charlotte came down here today?"

"Left ten minutes before you arrived to poke yer nose in," he grunted with a small laugh. "Practically begged me. I worked for that family for twenty-five years. *Twenty-five*! I served in the Falklands, y'know. Then Henry gets all high and mighty and shows me the door for drinking on the job. He couldn't keep hold of his staff, but I thought I was the exception until he gave me the boot two weeks ago. Wanted my job back at first but realised I was well shot of that place. I hope he rots in hell."

Andrew lifted his pint to the ceiling before gulping down the remaining contents. Julia edged forward, eager to hear more.

"Henry liked to fire people?"

"It was his favourite thing to do, lassie," Andrew said with a dark chuckle. "Gave the wee man power. He hardly cleared five feet in height. Napoleon complex right enough! Girls never last more than six months in that kitchen."

"And the family?" Julia asked, her heart racing. "What are they like?"

"A nightmare," he grunted, shaking his head heavily as he leant back in his chair to rest his head on the chunky frame of the oil painting. "That Charlotte is the worst, but she does have nerve, I'll give the lassie that. She stands her ground, but she's spoiled. Her brother is worse."

"And Mary?"

"The latest *Mrs McLaughlin*?" he snorted. "I've been there long enough to remember the *original Mrs McLaughlin*. She was the only one up to the job. The rest haven't held a candle to Sandra. Mary is running that place into the ground. I've never seen the place so quiet. Charlotte has been gunning for the lassie's job since Henry got rid of the last wife.

What was her name again? *Claire? Bridget?* It's hard to keep track. Now if you don't mind, I'm getting another drink, and I'd like it if you weren't here when I got back."

Andrew shuffled away from the table and towards the bar. Julia sat for a moment, absorbing the information she had just heard. She turned to Sue, and then to the bar. Andrew and the barmaid were both staring bitterly at them, and she knew they had overstayed their welcome.

"Why would Charlotte try so hard to give Andrew his job back?" she thought aloud. "And why on *that* morning? Why call him up there so early?"

"I don't know, and quite frankly, I don't care," Sue mumbled, linking arms with Julia and dragging her towards the exit. "I want a pedicure, a facial, and a nice long nap."

Julia didn't argue. Andrew had given her more than enough to think about, and as time ticked on, she found her attention directed more and more towards Charlotte McLaughlin.

CHAPTER 7

As the sun set on Seirbigh Castle, Julia found herself in her kitchen apron once more and pushing a trolley down the corridor towards the entrance hall. She glanced over her shoulder, where she could hear her gran loudly placing her dinner order with Blair. Looking down at the silver cloche, which contained haggis, neeps and tatties on the plate beneath it, she almost couldn't believe she had convinced Blair to let her take the food up to Charlotte alone.

She pushed through into the entrance hall, which aside from the roaring fire in the giant fireplace, was dark and deserted. She looked behind the reception desk and through to the office, but it was completely empty. She almost walked right by the fireplace and to the foot of the stairs, but something white fluttering on the stone slab in front of the flames caught her eye.

Leaving the trolley by the desk, she tiptoed over, glancing over her shoulder to make sure she was truly alone. She knew it was possible that somebody would be there any moment to turn on the lights, but her intrigue drove her forward.

She crouched down and stared at the corner of a white piece of paper that was charred and smouldering at the edges. She patted it with her hand and blew off the excess ash before lifting it up to her eyes. It appeared to be an official looking letter, but the only thing that was still visible was an address in Aberfoyle. Julia looked into the fire where she was sure she could see the ash remnants of a large stack of paperwork that had been dumped onto the flames. She knew it could be nothing, but she pocketed the piece of paper anyway.

Shortbread and Sorrow

With the trolley in hand, she made her way up to the landing and towards Charlotte's bedroom. She glanced at the miserable family portrait again and wondered if the little girl with the sad face could actually shoot her own father.

Julia knocked softly and waited a few seconds for Charlotte to summon her inside, before pushing carefully on the door, keeping her head bowed as she entered. She was relieved to see Charlotte sitting up in bed alone, in almost complete darkness aside from her bedside lamp. The heavy drapes were drawn, blocking out the last of the day's sunlight. Charlotte was wearing a pale pink silk robe, and her auburn hair was flowing down her chest, almost hitting the paperwork she was reading.

"I thought it was you I saw in here this morning," she said with a smile, the angry tone from earlier completely gone, and back to the welcoming one that had greeted her at check-in. "What are you doing in that apron?"

"I'm giving Blair a helping hand," Julia said with a smile as she pushed the trolley into the bedroom. "DI Fletcher wants us to stick around, so I thought I would help out."

"Oh," Charlotte said with a smile, a slight furrow in her brow. "Well, I guess I should thank you then."

Julia waved her hand to tell her that wasn't necessary. She pulled the cloche off the plate and looked down at the steaming slices of haggis, her stomach turning a little. Charlotte had insisted Blair cook it especially for her because it was her favourite meal, and even though it had taken Blair a trip into the village and nearly a full day of preparation, she had been too polite to refuse.

"Reading anything fun?" Julia asked, casting her gaze to the paperwork covering the sheets as she placed the plate on the nightstand.

"Just accounts," Charlotte said quickly before gathering them and dropping them into a cardboard box, which she swiftly shut. "Boring stuff."

Julia nodded and smiled, not wanting to admit to Charlotte that she knew what accounts looked like, and they weren't them. For a start, Julia didn't spot any numbers, just reams and reams of tiny letters covering many pages. If she hadn't spent the last two years wrapping her head around her own accounts for the café, Charlotte's lie might have washed over her.

"How are you feeling?" Julia asked as she poured a glass of water from the metal jug on the tray. "You've been through a lot these last couple of days."

As though a reminder that she should be grieving, Charlotte's expression suddenly dropped, and she looked into her lap, her hair falling over her face. She stared up at the ceiling as though to stop herself from crying, but no tears came forward. She scooped her long hair around one side, her robe slipping off her right shoulder. She wasn't wearing anything underneath, and Julia wouldn't have stared if it weren't for the dark black and purple bruise just below her right shoulder. When Charlotte caught her looking, she quickly pulled her robe together and grabbed the plate.

"That looks painful," Julia said as she passed Charlotte a knife and fork. "My gran swears by putting raw meat on a bruise, but I'm not sure if I quite believe that."

Charlotte forced a small laugh as she stared down at her haggis, her knife and fork clasped in one hand.

"I hit it on a door," she said quickly without missing a beat. "It looks worse than it feels. Why don't you take a seat, Julia?"

Charlotte motioned to the end of the bed as she cut into her haggis. Cooked mince and spices filled the room, turning Julia's stomach even more; eating was the last thing she wanted to do right now. She looked warily at the edge of the bed, and then to the door. She had promised Blair she would be back in a matter of minutes, but an invitation to talk to Charlotte, even if it was an unexpected one, fascinated Julia too much to turn it down. She perched on the edge of the bed.

"Tell me about yourself," Charlotte said. "You're from down south, right?"

"Peridale," Julia said. "It's a beautiful little village in the Cotswolds. I run a café there."

"A café?" she remarked, arching a brow before she put a forkful of the food into her mouth. "On your own?"

"I have help with the day-to-day side of things, but I run the business on my own."

"Not an easy thing to do," Charlotte said, glancing to the box. "I'm sure I have a lot to learn."

Julia followed her eye line to the box, dying to know what information the paperwork contained. She thought about the charred slip of paper in the front pocket of her apron and wondered if this box was next for burning.

"So you're going to be running things around here?" Julia asked, looking around the vast space. "It's a big castle for one woman. I thought Mary was the manager?"

"*She* thinks that too," she said with a devious smile. "She has no claim to this place. She might have been my father's wife, but she wouldn't have been for much longer. The lawyers have the relevant paperwork to prove the divorce was all but final. She's being *dealt* with."

Julia's stomach dropped. The sinister look in Charlotte's eyes as she took another mouthful of haggis unsettled her. Julia turned her attention to the window. Through the gap in the heavy drapes, the sun was setting on Scotland for another day. She had never felt further from home.

"Have you managed to get out and about?" Julia asked, making sure to gauge Charlotte's reaction. "The weather has been lovely. The fresh air might do you good."

Charlotte slowly chewed her food, her expression unwavering. There was a little glimmer in her eyes that told her that Charlotte knew she had been to the village to speak to Andrew. Julia forced her soft smile to remain while her heart trembled in her chest.

"I went into the village this morning," she replied flatly. "To speak to our ex-groundskeeper. I offered Andrew his old job back, but he was reluctant to take it."

"I thought his position had been filled by Blair's brother?" Julia asked. "I met him this morning. He seems like a nice man."

"That position is soon to become vacant," Charlotte said through a strained smile. "I'll let you go. You shouldn't spend your trip cooped up in that kitchen. Enjoy what we have to offer."

"I'm sure I'll have a chance before I leave," Julia said softly as she stood up. "Enjoy your dinner."

She closed her hands around the trolley and walked as quickly as she could out of the dark room. When she closed the door behind her, she realised she had stopped breathing entirely. Taking in a deep lungful of the musty castle air, she stared at the portrait on the wall again. Once more, she wondered if that little girl could be capable of murdering her father, and this time, her conclusion was less optimistic.

* * *

WHEN SHE WAS BACK IN THE DEPTHS OF the castle, Julia was relieved to see that Blair had finished serving Dot and Sue's dinner and was drinking a cup of tea while flicking through a gossip magazine. It was comforting to see her doing something normal for once.

"I thought you'd gotten lost," Blair exclaimed as she looked up from her magazine. "I was about to come looking for you."

"I had a little chat with Charlotte," Julia said, trying not to give away anything on her face. "I just think she's lonely."

Blair frowned a little, but to Julia's surprise, she didn't question her further, and she returned to her magazine.

Julia decided to take advantage of the quiet time to retrieve her phone from her bag. She pulled the slip of paper out of her pocket and opened up the internet browser. She hovered over the search bar, blankly looking down at the address. With a shake of her head, she put the slip of paper into her bag, closed down the browser, and did something more important.

"*Barker?*" Julia whispered into the phone as she pressed it against her ear. "It's Julia."

"*Julia!*" Barker exclaimed, the joy in his voice soothing her in an instant. "Enjoying the spa? I've wanted to call you all day, but I didn't want to ruin your relaxing time. How's Dot and Sue?"

"They're good," Julia said, pushing forward a

smile as she pinched between her eyes. "How are things there?"

"Everything is fine," he said. "We've just finished eating dinner. Jessie made us fish and chips."

"How's the café?"

"It's all fine," he said with a small chuckle. "You don't have to worry about a thing. Jessie has really stepped up to the plate. She's taking it all in her stride."

"And Mowgli?"

"He's on my knee right now."

An easy smile spread across Julia's face. She closed her eyes, and she could picture the scene as clear as day. Barker would be sitting in the seat nearest the fire, with the heat licking at his feet because he didn't like to wear socks in the house. Mowgli would be snoring softly, popping his head up every time Barker fidgeted. Jessie would be sitting at the opposite end of the room, her face buried in her new tablet, with a cup of peppermint and liquorice tea balanced dangerously on the chair arm. She would take a couple of sips, but she wouldn't finish the cup; she never did.

Sadness swept over Julia like a heavy tide she couldn't fight. She wanted nothing more than to be there with them.

"*Julia*?" Barker mumbled. "Are you still there?"

"I'm still here," she whispered. "Signal isn't great."

"I said that I'm taking Jessie on her first driving lesson tomorrow," Barker whispered down the handset. "I've upgraded my insurance premiums to cover everything."

She heard Jessie call out something in the background. It was no doubt a sarcastic remark about how she was going to be an excellent driver. Julia laughed to herself.

"Thank you for being there for her," Julia said, her heart fluttering. "I really appreciate it, and I know she does too."

"She's growing on me," Barker said, loud enough so that Jessie could hear him. "Like a bad rash."

Jessie called back something that Julia heard, but wouldn't repeat in the presence of Blair. She chuckled and looked over her shoulder, but she was still engrossed in her magazine.

"I'll let you get back to your relaxing week," Barker said, making Julia wish the conversation didn't have to end. "I miss you."

"I miss you too."

When she finally hung up, Julia stared down at her phone for what felt like a lifetime. Being away from Barker and Jessie made her realise how much she loved them both. Nothing tied any of them together aside from their desire to be there, and she knew that's what made them a family, dysfunctional or not.

The door to the kitchen opened, tearing her from her thoughts. She slipped her phone into her bag and was relieved to see Blair's brother, Benjamin, the very man she had wanted to talk to next.

"Evening, ladies," Benjamin said. "Anything tasty to eat, sis? I'm starving."

Blair closed her magazine and grabbed the shortbread that Julia and she had prepared in the gap between lunch and dinner. Julia and Benjamin pulled up a seat on either side of Blair at the counter while Blair teased the lid off the metal tartan tin. Benjamin didn't wait to grab a piece of the buttery and crumbly shortbread.

"Anyone would think you were Scottish," he mumbled through a mouthful, his eyes closed and content. "Delicious as ever."

"Julia can take the credit for that," Blair said proudly as she smiled at Julia. "She suggested a drop of vanilla extract, and it really punches through, don't you think?"

"Genius," Benjamin said with a nod. "You're quite the inventive baker, Julia."

Julia blushed as she reached out for a piece of shortbread. The room fell silent as they all enjoyed the baking. Julia swallowed quickly, deciding it was the perfect time to ask Benjamin the questions that had formed in her mind after speaking with Charlotte.

"What are your roles as a groundskeeper, Ben?" Julia asked casually. "There isn't much ground on this tiny island."

"It's a bit of a vanity title," he admitted with a smirk. "I have a little hut around the back of the castle where I work, but I'm more a maintenance guy. I fix up the castle best I can, light the fires, chop the firewood. That sort of thing. I make sure the castle is looking neat for when guests arrive. The family owns a little land beyond the bridge for the hunting, so I keep that in order too. It doesn't sound like a lot, but a castle this old takes a lot to keep it together."

"I don't doubt it's a difficult job," Julia said as she brushed the crumbs off her fingers. "I heard hunting is popular here? Do you get a lot of guests interested in that?"

"I haven't worked the hunting season yet, but I hear this place will be full of hunters in the coming months. Almost exclusively, according to Mary."

"Do you know much about hunting?"

"A little," he admitted. "I've been out and about with the rifle getting in some practice."

"I thought it was out of season?"

"For deer, yes," Benjamin said as he plucked another piece of shortbread from the tin. "But there are plenty of other animals scurrying around out there. Shrews, badgers, foxes, voles. Even the odd moose if you're lucky, but they rarely come this far south. I don't think I'll ever get used to shooting them down though, but Charlotte insisted I get used to it before the season starts. I'm not even sure if it's legal this time of year."

"Charlotte is a hunter?"

"She's more a mad woman with a gun," Benjamin said with a chuckle. "Shot at every shadow and piece of heather blowing in the breeze. She was trying to teach me, but her technique was so sloppy, I learned more by watching videos online."

"I bet that can cause some nasty injuries," Julia suggested casually as she played with a stray curl that had fallen from her bun. "I heard that guns like that can have some serious kickback."

Benjamin nodded as he looked down at the piece of shortbread in his left hand. He tossed it into his mouth before turning back to Julia.

"Are you thinking of giving it a go?" he mumbled through a mouthful. "I can take you out if you want."

"Thank you, but no thank you," Julia said, waving her hands in front of her. "I couldn't imagine shooting down an animal like that."

"Me neither," Blair agreed. "It's barbaric."

"It's *nature*," Benjamin said with a laugh. "The circle of life. *Hakuna Matata* and all that stuff."

"That's not what that means." Blair rolled her eyes and slapped his hand away from the tartan tin. She secured the lid, and much to her brother's dismay she put it back on the shelf with the other similar tartan tins. "I'm going to bed before Rory shows up and starts putting in crazy orders."

"Good idea," Julia agreed as she let out a yawn. "It's been a long day."

Julia slid off the stool and took off her apron. She paused and turned as Benjamin grabbed at the magazine. It slid out of his buttery fingers and off the table. He let out a groan before bending over to pick it up.

"Are you sticking around at Seirbigh Castle, Benjamin?" Julia asked, suddenly remembering what Charlotte had said about his position soon becoming vacant.

"I have no plans to leave," he said as he clumsily opened the magazine. "Why do you ask?"

"No reason," Julia lied, deciding it was best not to let the poor man know that he was likely to be fired from his job in favour of his predecessor if Charlotte had her way. "Goodnight."

Julia grabbed her bag and made her way up the winding stone stairs, through the empty dining room, and back towards the entrance hall. She stopped in her tracks when she spotted DI Fletcher slapping his hand repeatedly on the reception bell.

Julia dropped her head and attempted to hurry past him, but he stepped into her path, his hands in his pockets, and his youthful face filled with a smug expression.

"Off to bed so soon?" he asked, a well-groomed brow arching up his smooth forehead. "Or are you going back to the village to badger more of my witnesses?"

"I don't know what you mean," Julia said, looking him dead in the eyes. "*Excuse me*, DI Fletcher."

Shortbread and Sorrow

The young man stared down at her for the longest moment before finally relenting and stepping to the side. Julia rolled her eyes and pressed forward, ready to crawl into bed.

"Stay out of my investigation," he called after her as she pulled on the door leading to the second part of the castle. "A baker should know her place."

Julia glanced over her shoulder, her cheeks burning brightly. She could think of one hundred and one things she could say to the little boy in a man's suit at that moment. She shook her head, deciding it wasn't worth it. Letting the door swing in its frame, she hurried along the dark corridor, ready for her bed. If she had money in her pocket, she wouldn't have bet on Detective Inspector Jay Fletcher solving the case before she left the castle.

"Don't count me out just yet," she whispered to herself in the dark as she made her way up to her bedroom. "Don't count me out."

CHAPTER 8

Julia wandered around the castle in the dark, the scent of heather and moss deep in her nostrils. She tried to wiggle her nose to get rid of the smell, but she couldn't quite feel her face.

Something banged in the dark. Julia spun around, but the castle walls shifted around her. Ancient bricks crumbled away, dust and debris falling from every angle. She ran for her bedroom door, but it fell away with the rubble. Skidding to a halt, she looked beneath her as the floor fell away. She could see the loch below, rippling and moving, and completely black. It was inviting her in, but she knew she had to stay away.

A woman's shriek pierced through the dark. She crammed her hands up to her ears as she looked for a way out, but the floor continued to fall away. She stepped back and leant against the castle wall, but it betrayed her. As she fell towards the dark loch below, the sky swirling above her, the shrieking grew louder and louder, distracting her from her impending death.

Before she hit the loch, Julia bolted up in bed, sweat pouring down her burning face. As she panted for breath, she looked towards the piercing strip of sunlight seeping in through the heavy drapes. She realised it had just been a nightmare. She looked down at her bedroom floor, and it was still well and truly intact.

What was real, however, was the shrieking. Sue bolted up in bed, her hair matted and sticking up on one side. She looked around the room before landing on Julia.

"Was that you?" Sue whispered. "What time is it?"

Julia squinted at the small clock on her nightstand. It was only a little after six. The woman shrieked again, forcing them both out of bed and straight over to the far window.

Julia tore back the drapes, the bright morning sun blinding them both. She forced her eyes to stay open and adjust so she could see the commotion that was happening below. Squinting into the light, she saw a flash of red hair and a flash of black. She realised she was watching Rory attempting to drag Mary out of the castle.

"You have *no* right being here!" Rory cried as he hauled Mary towards the bridge. "Ex-wives don't have rights!"

"But I'm *not* an ex-wife," she screamed, thrashing against him unsuccessfully. "Henry was my husband!"

With his arms around her waist, Rory picked Mary up like she weighed no more than a bag of flour and carried her over to the bridge. For a moment, Julia thought he was going to throw her over the edge and into the murky loch below.

"It was a clever trick trying to destroy the divorce papers, but my father wasn't stupid enough to only have one copy," Rory cried, his Scottish accent growing thicker the louder he became.

"You're not getting a penny of his fortune or a single brick of this castle!"

Julia was about to suggest they go down and help her, but a loud and persistent knock at the door startled them both. Sue hurried over and let Dot in. Julia wasn't surprised to see her.

"What's that racket?" she cried, her hair a mess, and her eyes still half closed as she stumbled forward in her floor-length white nightie. "I can't see from my window."

"Rory is trying to kick Mary out," Sue whispered as Dot wrestled her way through the drapes to push in front of Julia.

"Didn't Henry already try that?" Dot exclaimed as she pushed her nose up against the glass. "She bounced right back like a boomerang and then a man turned up dead. If I were him, I wouldn't mess with her. She's *obviously* cursed."

"*Gran!*" Julia cried with a sigh. "Now isn't the time."

Rory dropped Mary on the edge of the bridge and pushed her in the direction of the cars parked on the other side. He said something to her that they couldn't hear, which elicited even more shrieking. Mary charged at him like an angry bull, but Rory was twice her size and built like a rugby player, even if he was wearing a sharp business suit.

"Just *go!*" he yelled, pushing her to the ground. "Nobody wants you here. Don't you get that?"

Mary let out a sob and melted into the ground. Rory hovered over her for a moment, before tossing something at her feet and turning on his heels with a shake of his head. As though nothing had happened, he adjusted his cufflinks and set off back towards the castle. As he walked, he glanced in the direction of Julia's window, and all three of them jumped back. She couldn't have been sure from her distance, but Julia was somehow certain he knew they had been watching.

Julia ran across the room and tore open her bag. She dug around for the slip of paper, and when she found it, she grabbed her phone and pulled up the internet browser once more. She quickly typed in the address, and she wasn't surprised to discover that the address belonged to a solicitor's office that specialised in divorces. It brought back memories of her own divorce, and her heart ached for Mary. Still in her nightgown, she hurried out of the room and made her way through the castle.

* * *

Shortbread and Sorrow

THE CLOUDS ABOVE WERE THICK AND pale, and fog had consumed the loch, blocking off the beautiful view and closing them in completely. Julia hurried through the castle entrance, the gravel underfoot scratching at her soles.

Hitching up her pale pink nightie, she walked as quickly as she could to where she had seen Mary, but she needn't have bothered. Mary hadn't moved an inch and was still slumped against the wall, sobbing into her hands. Julia hung back for a moment, clearing her throat to announce her presence.

Mary looked up at Julia, her brows tight and her eyes swollen. Her face was bare of any makeup, and she looked as though she hadn't been awake for long. Julia wouldn't have been surprised if Rory had dragged her out of bed intentionally in the early hours of the morning for maximum impact.

"*What?*" Mary barked, her voice coarse. "Come to gloat?"

"Not at all," Julia said softly, hurrying forward and crouching down. "Can I sit down?"

"Do what you want," Mary snapped, a little less harshly this time. "It's not like I own the place."

She let out a small bitter laugh before another flood of tears consumed her. Julia sat on the cold ground next to her and leant against the cold stone wall. She looked up in the direction of her bedroom, sure she could make out the shadows of Dot and Sue twitching at the drapes. She was almost certain they were talking about how she should have stayed out of things, but that wasn't Julia's style. She couldn't stand by and watch another woman cry; not after already doing that on her first day in the castle.

"I'm divorced," Julia whispered, nudging Mary's shoulder. "Only recently too. We separated well over two years ago, but I dragged out signing the papers for as long as I could. I didn't want the man back. I was happy to be rid of him, but I couldn't get past the notion of being a divorcee before I had even turned forty. Then I realised that was an old-fashioned way of thinking, and I've even met a great man who is ten times the man my husband was."

"I'm not divorced," she said as she wiped the tears from her cheeks. "I'm *widowed*. We might have worked things out."

Mary's sobs restarted, letting Julia know that Mary didn't believe that any more than she did. Julia slid her arm around her shoulders and pulled her in. To her surprise, Mary melted into her side like a child against its mother, despite Julia being the younger one.

"There's still life out there for you," Julia said,

squeezing hard. "Beyond this castle."

"So you're saying I should just give it up?" she snorted, tucking her hair behind her ears. "It's *rightfully* mine. The divorce was never finalised. Like you, I was dragging my heels, but Henry had had enough. He threw me out, and then – and then he was *murdered*. I loved him."

"There are kinder men to love."

Mary sniffled and looked hopefully at Julia. For the first time since she had arrived, Mary smiled at her, and it felt genuine. Julia immediately discounted any involvement in Henry's murder. She felt foolish for even doubting the sincerity of the poor woman's tears.

"I thought I was different," Mary said with a small laugh. "I knew I was *number four*, but I thought he was a good man."

"Doesn't it always start out that way?" Julia asked as she rested her head on the wall and looked up at the milky sky. "Mine packed all of my things into black bags, put them on the doorstep, changed the locks, and informed me with a note that we were over. He didn't even write it. It was his secretary's handwriting. That's who he left me for. She was ten years younger than me, and twenty pounds lighter. Blonde, too."

"Maybe all men aren't so different," Mary said with a small laugh. "I didn't want to believe the rumours, but the castle walls talk. I kept hearing that he was going behind my back with the guests and even the staff, but I didn't want to believe it. It was easier to pretend everything was okay and ignore the obvious, just to keep up the charade."

Julia knew that feeling all too well. Now that she had some distance from her own marriage, she knew she had been sucked in by his charm and wit, but the rest had been nothing more than a sham. She had happily played along if only to say she was in a happy marriage. She almost couldn't believe she had ever been that woman.

"What are you going to do now?" Julia asked carefully, glancing up to her bedroom window where they were still being watched.

"I'm going to fight," she said sternly as she wiped her nose with the back of her hand. "That man owes me that much, doesn't he?"

Julia didn't say anything. She hadn't asked for a penny during the divorce, even though Jerrad had more than a large pot of savings. She had wanted to get out with her hands clean and only take what she had earned for herself. Years of working in the cake production factory had given her just enough savings to set up her café and a little left over to put down a deposit on a mortgage for her cottage. She looked up at the castle, wondering if she would have acted any differently if the stakes were higher. She would like to think it wouldn't have made a difference, but she knew it was easy to say that on the other side.

"What about Charlotte and Rory?" Julia asked. "They're not going to give this up easily."

"They've wanted to get their grubby hands on this place for years," Mary said, suddenly sitting up straight and shaking off Julia's hand. "I need to see my lawyer. I'm not vanishing like they want. If those brats want a war, it's a war they've got."

Mary stumbled to her feet and turned to the castle. She inhaled the fresh morning air and closed her eyes as she tucked her long black hair behind her ears once more. She straightened out her black silk pyjamas and picked up a set of car keys that were on the ground, no doubt tossed at her by Rory.

"Why don't you come down to the kitchen for a cup of tea?" Julia suggested as she struggled up to her feet. "They never go down there. I'll even cook up some breakfast."

"I need to go," Mary said, looking to the end of the bridge where three cars were parked. "Those two are going to be doing everything they can to freeze me out. I need to catch up. I thought doing my job and acting like everything was normal might have been enough, but they're sneakier than that. I even tried burning the evidence of the impending divorce, but of course, they have copies! Henry was a clever man, but I'm clever too. They were letting me think I was safe here so they could pull the rug from under my feet, but the joke is going to be on them. The man was *my* husband. *I* was his next of kin."

"Didn't he have a will?"

"I was his *fourth* wife," Mary said as though it was evident. "I doubt that man has changed his will since his *precious* Sandra died. We were all just stand-ins on his arm, and I was one of the unlucky idiots to fall for it. Thank you, Julia. You've really given me some perspective."

Mary quickly hugged Julia before hurrying along the narrow bridge to the cars at the bottom. She jumped into a silver one and sped off into the distance, her tyres screeching and sending gravel flying as she did. Julia watched as she zoomed around the corner and disappeared into the hills. Turning back to the castle, she looked up to her bedroom window and sighed. She had a feeling in the pit of her stomach that she had made things worse, not better.

Shortbread and Sorrow

* * *

AFTER RETURNING TO HER ROOM AND explaining what had happened to Dot and Sue, Julia quickly dressed and set off towards the kitchen to help Blair with preparing the breakfast. On her way, she was surprised to see Charlotte behind the counter, looking as void of personality as she had on the day they had arrived, and even more surprised when Charlotte looked to Julia as though she had been expecting to see her.

"Ah, Julia," Charlotte said after quickly swallowing her tea and placing her mug under the counter. "If you're on your way down to the kitchen, you'll have to stop I'm afraid. I haven't been myself these last couple of days, and I didn't pause to think that you're not insured to work here. If anything happens, we'd be liable, and a lawsuit is the last thing we need right now. There's so much paperwork to sort out, and a funeral to plan."

"I'm a very careful cook," Julia insisted. "And suing people isn't my style. Honestly, I actually enjoy helping out."

"Even so, I can't take the risk," Charlotte said as she flicked through a book under the counter. "I'm going to have to insist you don't go anywhere near the kitchen, or I'm afraid I'll have to take some kind of action. I'd hate to see your gran and sister suffer for your actions."

Charlotte suddenly looked up at Julia, their eyes connecting for a brief second. Despite the reception friendly smile, Julia was in no doubt that Charlotte had just threatened her. Deciding against arguing, Julia turned back on her heels and headed back towards the door she had just come through. She couldn't help but think Charlotte was trying to stop Julia from speaking to Blair, and she didn't know why, but it only made her want to speak to her more.

"Oh, and Julia?" Charlotte called after her as she yanked on the door. "We're having a celebratory dinner tomorrow night in our private drawing room. It's a tradition my father was very keen on doing for our guests every Sunday night, and I would like to continue it, especially since we had new arrivals last night. I hope to see you and your family there at seven."

"I wouldn't miss it," Julia said without a second thought.

Julia yanked on the door and hurried along the corridor and towards the sweeping staircase up to her bedroom. She couldn't believe any daughter grieving for her father would be throwing a celebratory dinner only days after his murder. She was beginning to wonder if Charlotte had any human emotions after all.

"Where are you going?" Dot exclaimed when they met in the corridor on the floor of their bedrooms, a towel draped over her shoulder. "I thought you were helping Mary Poppins down in the cellar?"

"Charlotte has just informed me that I'm forbidden from going down there," Julia said with a sigh as she scratched the back of her head. "Something to do with insurance, but it sounded like an excuse to me. She's up to something."

"Well if she is, let it go!" Dot cried as she hooked her arm around Julia's. "We only have the weekend to enjoy the spa before we're back in Peridale and then we never have to think about this place again. I'm not taking no for an answer, young lady."

"Where's Sue?"

"Honking her guts up," Dot said with a roll of her eyes. "Food poisoning by the sounds of it. It turns out that your little friend isn't such a good cook after all. I've already called down and told them to count us out for breakfast. Turns out two couples checked in last night, so she'll have plenty more victims to poison with her cooking. Maybe it's best you stay away from her. I don't want her shoddy standards rubbing off on you. Sue said she'll join us when she's feeling better."

Julia glanced over her shoulder to her bedroom door as her gran dragged her down the corridor towards the staircase. Spending a day in the spa was the last thing she wanted to do, but she knew she didn't have much choice. She could try and sneak down into the kitchen to talk to Blair, but she was sure Charlotte and Rory would be keeping a watchful eye on the young girl all day.

She let her gran drag her down to the ground floor where the spa and pool were situated. Once on a bed, Julia picked a face sheet mask at random and allowed the kind woman to apply it. Thankfully for Julia, she didn't try to make small talk, which allowed her mind to really think.

She stared up at the wooden ceiling and tried to think of reasons Charlotte would want to keep her away from Blair. She wondered if her conversation with Mary had been seen by either of the siblings and if that was a possible reason, but she couldn't make a connection between the wife and the cook. She knew she could be clutching at straws, and the insurance could be a legitimate reason for keeping her out of the kitchen, but it didn't sit right with Julia. Charlotte might have had a pretty face and a sweet smile, but Julia was sure if she lightly scratched beneath the surface, she would uncover the young woman's dark insides very quickly.

Within a matter of minutes, Dot was already snoring under her slices of cucumber. Julia wondered if she was too harsh on Charlotte. She had, after all, just been orphaned, even if her relationship with her father didn't seem all that close. Julia wasn't particularly close to her own father, and her own mother had died when she was a little girl, but she couldn't empathise with Charlotte despite their similarities. She knew it was very possible for people to hide their pain from the world, but Julia didn't feel anything from Charlotte, other than coldness.

Before she could delve any deeper, Sue shuffled into the spa, her face a pale shade of green. She gratefully accepted a white robe and took the bed next to Julia. Without saying a word, she tossed her head back and inhaled deeply.

"Food poisoning?" Julia asked.

"Something like that," Sue mumbled. "I can't wait to be out of this place. What are you doing here, anyway?"

"It's a long story," Julia whispered, sitting up and turning to Sue. "I've been banned from the kitchen, but I need to figure out a way to get down there. I'm pretty sure Charlotte and Rory are going to be keeping watch."

"What's that got to do with me?" Sue groaned.

"I need to get a message to Blair so she can meet me," she continued quietly as she flung her legs around the side of the bed, letting her sheet mask slide off her face. "I think she knows something crucial to cracking this case, even if she doesn't realise it. I'll look less suspicious if you're with me."

"You'll look less suspicious if you just stay here and let them pamper you," Sue whined, her eyes clenching and her bottom lip protruding.

"Fine," Julia said as she tugged off her robe and tossed it over the bed. "I'll just go on my own. I just thought it would be fun to have some sister time that wasn't spent horizontal in a coma with gunk on our faces."

Julia turned on her heels and walked towards the entrance. Out of the corner of her eye, she spotted a notepad and a pen on the glass reception desk. She tore off a piece and quickly scribbled down a note before pocketing it. As she headed to the door, she was surprised to see Sue quickly tearing off her robe.

"You know emotional blackmail is below the belt," Sue whispered as they both quickly headed down the corridor and towards the entrance hall. "What did you have in mind?"

"Let's just take a stroll around the island and see where it takes us."

CHAPTER 9

The moment they stepped out of the castle, Sue gasped and grabbed Julia's hand. They took a careful step forward, but the fog had rolled in from the loch, meaning she could barely see more than a couple of steps ahead of them.

"Maybe we should go back," Sue begged, tugging on Julia. "It doesn't look *safe*."

"It'll be fine," Julia said, pulling Sue forward.

"We just need to watch our step."

"What are we even doing out here?"

"Looking for someone."

They carefully walked down the gravel slope towards the bridge, taking small baby steps as the cool fog consumed them. Julia looked back at the castle, but it was nothing more than a dark smudge in a chalky sea of white.

Instead of taking the bridge across the loch, they stepped down onto a small winding path that circled the edge of the tiny island. Julia gulped hard as she looked down into the murky surface of the water, which would swallow her up without a second thought if she took one wrong step. The bank sloped up towards the base of the castle, heather and lumpy rock covering its surface. The earthy tones of the spiky plant didn't smell as delightful since her dream.

"I don't like this," Sue whispered, her fingers tightening around Julia's. "I don't like this *one bit*."

The path curved and Julia suspected they were walking around the back of the castle. She looked up at the bank and kept her eyes peeled for a hut, but she wasn't sure she would see it even if it was right in front of her. She looked back, but the bridge had vanished from sight.

The path suddenly took a sharp incline away from the water, relaxing Julia a little. Through the fog, she could see that they were walking back towards the castle. When the ground levelled out, the path suddenly cut off, joining in with the bumpy land. Despite Sue dragging her heels, Julia pressed forward, heading towards the blur of the castle. When they finally reached it, she pressed her hands against the cool stone, reassured that she was going the right way.

They followed the castle walls and came to the dining room. Julia peered through the windows, but it was dark and empty. She had hoped Blair was there so she could somehow call her over so they didn't have to go any further.

They hurried past the tall windows and followed the building around. A thumping sound pierced through the fog like a cracking whip, startling them both. Sue pulled back, but Julia pulled her towards the sound. She was surprised when she came out into a clear stone courtyard. They stepped inside, turning back to watch as the thick fog rolled by.

She let out a thankful breath when she saw Benjamin chopping logs of firewood against an old tree stump. Despite the chilly morning, he had forgone a shirt so that his sweat-glistening and lightly haired chest was on display. To Julia's surprise, he was chopping the logs of wood with the sheer force of his left arm, his right tucked neatly behind his back.

"*Wow*," Sue whispered. "That's *strength*."

Benjamin looked up, the axe swinging and missing the log. It buried into the tree stump. He wiped the sweat from his forehead before picking up his shirt and pulling it on.

"It's sweaty work," he said with a twinkling smile. "You ladies are braver than me to venture into that fog. I'm waiting for it to clear."

Sue gave Julia an '*I told you so*' look, but Julia pursed her lips, telling her not to bother saying anything. She let go of her sister's hand and walked towards Benjamin, looking up at the castle as she did. Tall walls rose high on all sides, the different parts of the castle joining together. Julia tried to work out where she was in relation to the rest of the building, but she couldn't quite figure out where they had walked in the fog. At the end of the courtyard, she spotted the stone hut Benjamin had told her about.

"We were actually coming to find you," Julia said with a soft smile. "I hope we're not interrupting."

"Not at all," he said as he swung the axe down again. "This is my last log. What can I do for you?"

"I was wondering if you could pass a message on to Blair?" Julia asked as she retrieved the handwritten note from her pocket. "I've been banished from the kitchen, and I really wanted to talk to her."

"Couldn't you just wait for one of her breaks?"

"I want to talk to her *away* from the castle," Julia whispered, looking around, suddenly becoming aware of all of the windows. "I think she knows something that might help unlock the secret to Henry's murder, and I think Charlotte knows that and she's trying to keep us apart."

Benjamin took the note and opened it, his brows curiously pinching together. He quickly read the note that asked Blair to meet Julia in a café in Aberfoyle after she had finished for the day, along with Julia's phone number.

"I thought you were a baker?" he asked with a little smirk as he pocketed the paper. "You're acting like some kind of detective."

"She *is* a baker," Sue said, joining Julia by her side. "She just seems to *forget* that every time a murder happens near her, which is happening increasingly more often than I would like to admit.

Gran thinks she's the harbinger of death."

"She does?" Julia exclaimed, turning to her sister.

"Well, she's not going to say that to your *face*, is she?" Sue mumbled with a shrug.

"I'll pass on the note," he said with a wink. "You don't think my sister is in danger, do you?"

"I don't know," Julia admitted, not wanting to lie to the man. "But Charlotte appears to think it's crucial to keep us apart."

"*Or* it is just the insurance?" Sue whispered.

"Or that," Julia said with a sigh. "But it's all just a little suspicious."

"I'll keep an eye on her and an ear to the ground," Benjamin said as he started tossing the logs into a wheelbarrow. "If you want to get back into the castle, there's a door that leads to the drawing room. It's not really for guests, but I'm sure I can make an exception with the fog. I wouldn't feel right letting you walk along that path. It's not safe at the best of times."

Sue rolled her eyes and pouted before linking arms with Julia and following Benjamin across the courtyard. Julia looked up at the many windows to her right, suddenly realising they were part of the family's quarters above the entrance hall. She gulped, hoping she had been quiet enough to not betray herself.

Benjamin walked them to a stone wall, forcing Julia and Sue to look questioningly at each other. To their equal surprise, Benjamin pulled on the bricks, and a piece of the wall the exact size of a door opened onto a dark corridor.

"Follow that down to the bottom, and you'll come out in the drawing room," he said as he held the heavy stone door open.

"A secret passageway?" Sue asked, her face lighting up. "I *knew* it!"

"The castle is full of them," Benjamin said with a smirk. "Makes my job a lot easier. There's a peephole in the door at the other side. Just make sure nobody is watching when you slip through."

Sue clenched her hand around Julia's once more, and they stepped into the dark. With one final goodbye, Benjamin pushed the door shut, concealing them within the walls of the castle. Just like when walking through the fog, she took tiny steps through the stuffy and narrow corridor. Mildew and decay tickled her nostrils.

"This is *so* cool," Sue whispered. "I *told* you there would be secret passages."

"Explains how Charlotte managed to get across

the castle so quickly if she *did* kill her father."

"*If?*" Sue mumbled. "I thought you were certain it was her?"

"I'm certain of nothing until I have all of the facts," she whispered back, turning pointlessly to her sister in the pitch black. "It's just a hunch."

A narrow stream of light illuminated the dusty air, letting them know they had reached the door into the drawing room. Julia let go of Sue's hand and pushed her eye up against the tiny circle in the wall.

She saw an explosion of mahogany through the tiny gap. A grand banqueting table stretched out down the centre of the room, a crystal chandelier as big as Julia's car dangling over it. The walls were lined high with dark bookshelves, which were crammed with thick leather-bound volumes. On the other side of the room, she spotted the giant ornate doors, which would lead them back to the safety of the castle.

"Looks clear," she whispered back to Sue. "Try to be quiet."

Julia pushed carefully on the door. It felt heavy under her hands, but it eased forward, flooding the darkness with light. She held it open enough for Sue to slip through, before squeezing through herself.

She closed the door, surprised to see it was a bookshelf on the other side. She smiled to herself, feeling like she was fulfilling some kind of childhood fantasy to have her own bookcase door that led to a secret room.

"*Get down*," Sue whispered, yanking Julia to the ground and behind a red Chesterfield sofa. "*We're not alone.*"

She pointed over the top of the sofa to the large bay window looking out over the loch. Julia peered over the edge, instantly bobbing back down when she saw a flash of red hair over the top of a high-backed leather armchair pointed in the direction of the foggy view.

"*Charlotte*," Julia mouthed to Sue. "*Stay here.*"

Julia wriggled free of Sue's grasp and crawled out from behind the couch. On her hands and knees, she scurried forward like a cat, pausing behind a side table. She peered around the corner of the mahogany unit, instantly ducking back when she saw the profile of the person sitting in the other chair. Julia looked around and spotted another Chesterfield sofa positioned behind them. Without a second thought, she hurried forward and pushed her back up against the hard sofa. She strained her ears, but she needn't have bothered. Charlotte wasn't concealing her conversation behind a whisper.

"I need you to get *rid* of her," she said firmly, no doubt staring out into the fog. "She's *trouble*."

"I'm done wi' this," the thick Scottish accent of Andrew replied. "I've done yer dirty work, lassie. Find somebody else to *use*."

"Don't act like you're not being paid for your services, Mr McCracken," Charlotte said, the chair creaking under her. "Seirbigh Castle will be mine in a matter of days if you have done what you said, and you will get what was promised to you."

"'Course I did what I said," he growled back. "But you told me that was the last thing."

"You've come this far, Mr McCracken," Charlotte replied as she stood up. "Don't stumble at the final hurdle. The girl is trouble and you know it's going to be difficult to legally fire her considering the circumstances. Besides, she knows too much. She could speak out. I want her out of Seirbigh Castle before all of the paperwork is official. Now that Mary is gone, *she's* the final thorn in my side. Do what you have to do, Mr McCracken, and welcome back to the family. You should never have been disposed of in the first place."

Footsteps clicked on the polished wood floors, sending Julia scurrying back behind the side table.

She caught Sue's eyes, who was desperately waving for Julia to come back. Julia waited until she heard the door close before dashing back to her sister.

"Have you gone *crazy*?" Sue whispered angrily. "I hope that was worth it."

"It was," Julia replied. "Let's get out of here."

Julia grabbed Sue's hand and still keeping low to the ground, they hurried towards the doors on the other side of the room. Before she reached it, she glanced over to Andrew as he reached around the side of the chair to top up his whisky from the glass decanter.

They slipped through the door, coming out facing the dining room. It was still dark and empty, but Rory was now sitting at the closest table with his back to them, hunched over something. Julia stopped in her tracks and tried to peer around him to see what he was doing, but all she could conclude was that he was writing something.

"Ah! There you are!" the voice of DI Fletcher made them both spin around. "I've been looking for you everywhere. Can you gather in the entrance hall with the other guests, please?"

"Why?" Julia asked as Rory turned to see what was happening.

"*Now*, Miss South," he ordered as he stepped to

the side and motioned towards the double doors leading through to the reception area. "Rory, do you know where your sister is? I need to speak with you both in private."

Julia reluctantly let Sue drag her down the corridor, without taking her eyes away from DI Fletcher. Just from the look on his face, she could tell he wasn't gathering them to give them good news. She wondered if he could have possibly cracked the case and have a suspect in custody. It seemed unlikely, but it would be a relief to put an end to the whole affair.

They joined their gran by the reception desk, where she was staring sternly at the new guests, still in her white robe and bright green facemask.

"Where have you two been?" she snapped when she noticed them.

"We went for a walk," Julia said, hoping the truthful part of that statement made up for the fact she was keeping quiet about the outcome of that walk. "What's going on?"

"I don't know," she said with a sigh. "But it's keeping me from my depleting spa time. DI CryBaby gathered us all here to tell us something important. I wonder if he's just got his first chest hair and wants to share the news."

The two new couples both snickered at Dot's joke, but she stared at them sternly, letting them know they didn't have permission. Julia smiled reassuringly at the two young couples. Just from their confusion and lack of interest in the collapsed bannister above them, she could tell they had no idea that they were standing directly on the scene of a man's murder.

The double doors opened, and DI Fletcher walked in, followed by Rory and Charlotte. Charlotte was sobbing heavily, her face buried in her brother's chest, and Rory was trying his best to comfort her, his expression solemn and his eyes vacant. Julia's stomach turned uncomfortably.

"A car was found crashed an hour ago on the road to Aberfoyle," DI Fletcher announced. "The driver, Mary McLaughlin, the manager of this hotel, was found dead behind the wheel."

A gasp ricocheted through the small crowd, but Charlotte's increased sobs drowned it out. Rory wrapped his arms around his sister and pulled her in.

"I saw her drive away this morning!" one of the new men explained. "She was screeching outside. It woke us up!"

"*Me too!*" the woman in the other couple said with a nod. "Drove off like a *madwoman*."

"We saw her too," Dot volunteered. "Didn't we girls? Julia even went down and spoke to her."

Guilt consumed Julia. She looked down at the ground, unable to look the young DI in the eyes. Why hadn't she tried harder to stop Mary from driving off? She tried to think of what could have caused the woman to crash, but Charlotte's cries were distracting her.

"I'm going to need to take statements from each of you," he said, already pulling a notepad out of his pocket. "Since you can't seem to stay out of things, why don't we start with *you*, Miss South?"

CHAPTER 10

Julia followed DI Fletcher back into the dining room. He pulled up a seat at the table Rory had been sitting at, but the paperwork he had been working on had already vanished.

"You know they're faking that grief?" Julia asked as she sat uninvited across the table from DI Fletcher. "Neither of them showed that much emotion when their own father was shot down. Find the gun yet?"

"We're doing our best to find the murder weapon," he said as he flicked through his notepad to a fresh page. "Why don't you start at the beginning?"

"Your best isn't good enough." Julia clung onto the edge of the table, leant through the dim light, and looked the DI dead in the eyes. "A woman has *unnecessarily* died."

The DI arched a brow, a slight smirk pricking the corners of his lips. He pulled the lid off his pen, but he didn't write anything down. Instead, he just continued to stare at Julia as though he was a mixture of amused and irritated by her behaviour. It reminded her of the way Barker had looked at her when they had first met, but she doubted the young DI in front of her contained any of the same humility when he clocked off at the end of the day. Her chest tightened just thinking of Barker; she wanted nothing more than to see his face at that moment.

"We have no reason to believe it was anything but a tragic accident," he said, turning the pen upside down to tap furiously on the table surface. "Those roads are dangerous at the best of times without the added difficulty of driving through fog.

Mary McLaughlin wouldn't be the first woman to succumb to those roads."

"*Woman?*"

"Turn of phrase, Miss South," he replied through a strained smile. "I assure you I meant *nothing* by it, but the point still stands. Mary skidded off the road on a tricky turn and crashed through the barrier wall."

"If you analyse the car, I'm sure you'll find some tampering," Julia said firmly as she sat up and turned to the thick fog outside. "Cut brakes, perhaps?"

"There wasn't much left of the car," he said as he tugged at his collar. "Or of Mary. On a road that quiet, there's no telling how long the fire raged for."

Julia closed her eyes and forced back the tears. Why hadn't she insisted Mary stay behind? She tried to reassure herself that she couldn't have known this would happen, but after everything she had heard so far today, a second murder wasn't as surprising as she would have liked to have believed.

"Charlotte *is* involved," Julia said. "I heard her talking to the ex-groundskeeper, Andrew McCracken, moments before we bumped into you. If fact, I'm sure Andrew is still there. I haven't seen him leave yet, have you?"

Shortbread and Sorrow

Julia jumped up and hurried across the dining hall to the drawing room. She pushed confidently on the heavy double doors, but she didn't need to take a step into the room to know the chair was empty. She rushed over, but the only evidence Andrew had even been there was the drained whisky tumbler and the almost empty decanter.

"I can't see anybody, Miss South," he said as he followed her into the room, wincing as he scratched at the side of his head with his pen. "Why don't you sit down and tell me about this conversation?"

"Charlotte was asking Andrew to get rid of somebody, and she alluded to the fact he had already done it once. She mentioned Mary was now gone to leave her to take control of the castle." Julia turned to the bookcase she had slipped through, and a light bulb sparked above her head. "*The secret passage!*"

The DI walked over to the armchair and picked up the decanter. He lifted off the lid and gave it a sniff, but Julia was already running across the room. She stared at the bookcase she was sure concealed the hidden door.

"Secret passage?" he called after her as he weaved in and out of the furniture to catch up. "Do you realise how ridiculous you sound right now?"

"It's true," Julia said, scrambling at the books for

a secret lever or switch. "It's *right* here. It leads out into the courtyard. He could be halfway back to the village by now."

"Who?"

"*Andrew!*"

"What does Andrew McCracken have to do with Mary McLaughlin's death?" he asked with an exasperated sigh. "Please, Miss South, try to stay on topic."

"Aren't you listening to me?" she cried, turning away from the bookcase and back at the DI. "Charlotte is pulling all of the strings. She shot her father and had Mary killed. She's desperate to run this castle. Her very words were *'whatever it takes'*. She's ruthless."

"Do you have any evidence, aside from a conversation you claim to have overheard?"

"I *did* overhear it," she snapped. "Sue was there. She'll account for the secret passage too. Benjamin, the new groundskeeper, told me the castle was full of them. I suppose that's how Charlotte managed to be in the opposite part of the castle when her father was discovered. She must have slipped away and waited until witnesses could see her walking onto the scene."

"You're not making any sense."

"I'm making *perfect* sense!" she cried, her hands disappearing up into her curls. "Why aren't you writing any of this down?"

He sighed and pinched between his brows as he took a seat on the red Chesterfield Julia and Sue had been hiding behind not that long ago.

"Just tell me what happened when Mary drove away from this castle?" he asked, opening his notepad again. "And *please* stick to the *facts*."

Julia reluctantly sat next to him. She ran through the story of being awakened by the shrieking and seeing Rory pushing her out of the castle. She told him all about their conversation, and how Mary had insisted on going to see her lawyer. When she was finished, she looked down at the polished floor, Mary's tears ringing through her ears.

"Thank you, Miss South," he said as he slapped the notepad shut. "You've been very helpful."

"Have I?" she mumbled with a strained laugh. "I could hand you the killer with a stack of evidence and you would instantly dismiss me."

"If you hand me the killer with a stack of evidence, I'll owe you a drink, Miss South," he said with a wink as he stood up. "But until then, your witness statements are more than enough."

The DI turned on his heels and strode

confidently out of the drawing room, his black trench coat fluttering behind him. She turned back to the bookshelf, wondering how things had turned so peculiar so quickly. Standing up, she walked over to the window and stared out at the loch through the fog. It was growing thicker by the second, keeping them from the rest of the world. Seven hour drive or not, it was more than tempting to jump into her trusty Ford Anglia and drive back to Peridale.

Deciding she was going to have a lie down in her bedroom while DI Fletcher spoke to Dot, Sue, and the others, Julia abandoned the drawing room, but not without looking back at the bookshelf once again. Her stomach squirmed uncomfortably at the thought of the peephole staring directly at her within the mass of leather-bound books. All of a sudden, she had the unnerving feeling she was being watched, and perhaps had been the whole time.

Shaking out her curls, she pulled on one of the ornate doors, stepping out into the corridor just as DI Fletcher appeared with Sue behind him. Before the door closed, she spotted Charlotte and Rory sitting at the bottom of the stairs, still putting on a performance for the rest of the guests. One of the new women was even trying her best to comfort them.

DI Fletcher and Sue walked past her, both giving her very different looks. DI Fletcher's said '*go away*', and Sue's said '*please stay*'. They both slipped into the drawing room, no doubt walking to the seats by the window to prevent eavesdropping. Turning to the empty dining hall, Julia had a better idea than listening in on the interview. With Charlotte and Rory otherwise occupied, she set off weaving between the tables and towards the kitchen.

* * *

JULIA CREPT DOWN THE WINDING STONE steps, her fingers dragging along the cold wall to steady her. She checked her watch, surprised that it was still only a little after nine. So much had happened since being awoken by Mary at six that morning, it felt like she had fit an entire day into just a few short hours.

Forcing herself not to think about Mary's crash, she reached the bottom of the stairs and peered through the round window in the door. She was relieved to see Blair alone in the kitchen, leaning over the stove as she moved bacon around in a pan with one hand, while she stirred baked beans with the other. She took a step back and wiped sweat from her rosy forehead, her eyes clenched tightly shut. Julia didn't know how anybody could expect this young girl to juggle the cooking for an entire castle on her own.

She was about to push on the door to help Blair finish preparing breakfast, but she stopped herself when Blair tore off her apron and tossed it on the table. She was wearing a khaki green wool jumper underneath it, rolled up at the sleeves. She dragged the sleeves down and began pulling it over her head. As she did, her white T-shirt slid up with it. Julia let out a small gasp when she saw the small, yet definite bump protruding out of Blair's stomach.

Almost out of sheer shock, she hurried into the kitchen, startling Blair as she pulled the jumper over her face. She tossed it onto the table and quickly yanked her shirt down, turning away from Julia as she loosely tied her apron around her waist, just as it had been every other time Julia had seen her.

"You're pregnant?" Julia asked, her voice barely above a whisper.

"You shouldn't be down here," Blair mumbled, her cheeks burning brightly as she flipped the bacon. "Charlotte has forbidden it. You're going to get me in trouble."

"You're *pregnant!*" Julia repeated, taking a step

forward.

Blair turned to face Julia, hovering over the frying pan with the metal spatula in her hand. They stared at each other for what felt like an eternity, neither of them knowing what to say. The stare was only broken when Blair yelped and tossed the burning hot spatula into the pan. Clutching her burnt hand tightly, she stepped back and immediately began crying. Julia hurried forward and turned off the stove. She took the young girl into her arms, who wrapped her arms around her shoulders, clutching onto her tightly. Through the apron, Julia could feel the tiny life pushing up against her.

"It's going to be okay," Julia whispered as she stroked the back of Blair's head.

"You can't tell anyone," she said as she pulled away from the hug, her pale cheeks tear-stained and her nose glistening. "Please, miss. *Promise* me you won't say anything."

"I promise."

"I haven't even told Ben yet," she said as she tried to suppress her sobs. "They'll fire me if they find out. They've done it before. I can't afford to lose this job. We both send money to our mam back home. She wouldn't survive without it."

Blair walked over to the sink, cramming one

hand under the cold tap as she wiped her tears with the other. Julia did the only thing she knew what to do. She flicked on the kettle, grabbed two cups, and pulled two peppermint and liquorice tea bags from the box she had given to Blair.

When the kettle boiled, she filled the cups and placed them on the counter. Blair gratefully accepted the tea. Staring into space, she hugged it tight to her chest as the weight of the world pushed down on her. Julia had to remind herself the girl was only nineteen.

"I need to finish breakfast," Blair said without moving, her eyes still wide. "Charlotte always eats later on a Saturday because she likes to sleep in on the weekends. I had the four new guests this morning, so I'm already running late."

"I don't think she's going to be thinking about breakfast," Julia said carefully. "Mary died this morning."

"*Died?*" Blair furrowed her brow tightly, suddenly turning in her seat. "How?"

"She crashed her car driving away from the castle this morning. I spoke to her just before it happened. The police seem to think it was an accident."

"You don't?"

"Do you?" Julia asked, arching a brow.

"Considering what happened to Henry, I don't think there are any accidents around here anymore. Everything has been happening very deliberately and when it's supposed to."

"I'm not sure what you mean," Blair whispered as she lifted the cup to her lips.

"I think you do," Julia replied, putting her cup down. "Or you don't realise you do. I overheard Charlotte talking earlier today, and I didn't understand what she meant at the time, but I think I do now. I think she knows you're pregnant. She asked Andrew to get rid of you."

"Get *rid* of me?" Blair echoed, the shake in her voice obvious. "What does that mean?"

"I don't know, but she wants this castle, and she is doing whatever she can to get it. She got rid of Mary, and I think you're next. She seems to think you know something that could derail her plans."

Blair looked down into her cup without blinking. Julia knew Blair knew exactly what she was talking about.

"I don't know anything," Blair mumbled, placing the cup on the table and hurrying back over to the stove. "I really need to get on with this before Charlotte calls down."

"Didn't you just hear what I said?"

"This has *nothing* to do with you," Blair snapped bitterly, casting an angry look over her shoulder at Julia. "You're just a guest here. You get to go back to your café in two days, and I have to stay here. If Charlotte is going to fire me, I need to work as hard as I can to try and change her mind. I can't bring my baby into this world without a penny to my name."

She placed her hand momentarily on her stomach, outlining the shape of the tiny barely-there bump. Julia could feel every part of Blair's frustration and anger radiating from every pore in her body, but despite her warning, she felt there was nothing she could actually do to improve the girl's situation.

"Just be careful," Julia whispered as she passed, resting a hand on Blair's shoulder. "This family is dangerous."

Blair shrugged off her hand and focussed on cooking Charlotte's breakfast as though nothing had sunk in. Sighing to herself, Julia reluctantly pulled on the kitchen door. She cast an eye through the tiny round window before she set off up the winding staircase. Blair lifted her hands up to her eyes and sobbed silently for a moment before shaking her head, picking up the spatula, and flipping the bacon once more.

"Julia?" a voice from the dark startled her.

Julia spun around to see Benjamin. She let out a relieved laugh, glad it wasn't Charlotte or Rory.

"I was just about to give your note to Blair," he said, pulling the letter from his pocket. "Is everything okay?"

"There's no need." Julia grabbed the note from Ben. "I've spoken to her. Can you just keep an eye on her for me? I don't think she appreciates me sticking my nose in, but I'm worried about her."

"Of course," he said quickly. "I always do. She's my little sister."

Julia thanked him with a smile before stepping around him. She hurried up the winding staircase and back through to the dining room. The fog had started to clear, but only to be replaced with a miserable grey sky.

Wondering if Sue was finished with her interview, she pushed her ear up to the door. She strained her hearing, but it was in vain. She looked ahead to the sunroom, where Charlotte and Rory were standing by the window and looking out at the clearing fog. They were both talking in whispers, the amateur dramatic tears from earlier having stopped entirely.

As she walked back to the entrance hall, Julia felt

the sands of time slipping away. She had less than two days to get to the bottom of this mystery before she could head home to Peridale with a clear conscience.

CHAPTER 11

The next morning at breakfast, Julia wasn't surprised when Blair ignored her entirely, only nodding when Julia put in her order for poached eggs on toast. Dot and Sue didn't seem to notice, so she decided against letting them in on Blair's secret. She had promised after all, even if that promise didn't make much difference in the grand scheme of things anymore.

After breakfast, Julia let Sue drag her to the spa one last time, if only to use the quiet time to properly think about everything. No matter how many different theories she pieced together about what had really happened to Henry and Mary McLaughlin, something didn't sit right every time. Her mind kept landing back on Charlotte, but her vision was clouded, and she knew she was missing vital clues concerning the reasoning behind the murders.

After her facial and shoulder massage, which she had enjoyed more than she had expected to, she wasn't surprised to see DI Fletcher sniffing around the castle once more. She was, however, surprised to see Andrew McCracken stacking the fire with logs a little before lunch, as though he had never been fired in the first place. When he walked past her, Julia tried her best to make eye contact with the man to see his true intentions, but he appeared to be avoiding her at all costs.

Above Andrew's apparent return to work, Julia was even more surprised to learn from one of the other guests that the dinner in the drawing room was still happening as scheduled that night, despite what had happened to Mary. Even though she wouldn't put anything past Charlotte at this point, she didn't quite understand how she could transition from grieving stepdaughter to gracious host in the space of a day.

"I haven't seen a single man in a kilt yet," Dot complained as she settled into a chair in the sunroom with a cup of tea. "I wanted to check Jessie's theory about the underwear. Despite that, this trip has been rather lovely."

"Ignoring the two deaths," Sue whispered as she peeled the wrapper off one of the cupcakes Blair had brought them.

"Everybody dies, sweetheart!" Dot exclaimed loudly, turning the heads of the couple who were enjoying the view on the other side of the room. "It doesn't mean I can't *relax*! I've had at least one of every facial and massage on the menu, and I feel remarkable for it. Feel how soft my skin is."

Dot crammed her hand in front of Sue's face, who recoiled before reluctantly giving it a stroke.

"Like a newborn's behind," Sue mumbled.

"We need to do this more often," Dot said, sighing contently as she turned back to look out at the clear loch. "I've really enjoyed this time alone with my two favourite granddaughters."

"We're your *only* granddaughters," Sue said.

"And that's why you're my favourites," she

teased with a wink. "Are you okay, Julia? You look distant."

Julia broke her gaze from the bank across the loch and turned to her gran, forcing a smile. She nodded, unsure if she had the energy to deny it. The truth was, she was distant, and she didn't know how her gran was so oblivious to what was going on in the castle. Every fibre of her being was telling her something bad was going to happen very soon, like an orchestra rising to its final crescendo.

"I think she's just missing Barker," Sue answered for her when she noticed Julia's lack of response. "I know I'm missing my Neil. Do you think we'll be able to drive into the village on the way home and pick up some souvenirs? I promised I'd bring him something."

"Sure," Julia replied, souvenirs the last thing on her mind. "Is that Benjamin?"

She stood up and walked over to the window, squinting at the mossy bank ahead. Benjamin was walking amongst the heather in his usual green Barbour jacket. With Andrew apparently being back she had assumed Benjamin had already been given his marching orders. She had even tried to put Blair's distance down to that, and not what had transpired yesterday in the kitchen.

"Looks like him," Sue said.

"Who's Benjamin?" Dot asked. "Whoever he is, he looks like a fine specimen of a man."

"He is," Sue said, blushing a little, no doubt remembering him with his shirt off the morning before. "He's the cook's brother."

"I wonder if he's as miserable as her," Dot exclaimed, catching the attention of the couple again. "My stomach hasn't felt right all week!"

"I thought you said you'd been relaxed?" Julia mumbled over her shoulder, her defence of Blair automatic by this point, despite being blanked that morning. "Why have *two* groundskeepers?"

"*Huh?*" Dot replied, arching a brow. "Why does it matter?"

"Because we're in a castle that has been running with a skeleton staff since we arrived. Why rehire the old groundskeeper and keep his replacement around?"

"Maybe because there's a lot of ground?" Dot suggested with a roll of her eyes. "Honestly, Julia, I don't know why you care so much about these things."

"Because somebody has to," she said before pulling her phone from her pocket and walking out of the sunroom.

As she scrolled to Barker's number, she walked past the dining hall and straight through the open doors to the drawing room. She was relieved to see it empty. She pushed the phone against her ear, closed her eyes, and waited. Barker picked up on the last ring.

"*Hello?*" he called down the phone. "*Julia?*"

"It's me," she said, a smile flooding her face. "I just wanted to hear your voice."

"*What?* I can't hear you? *Jessie!* Take that turn! *Slow down!*"

Julia heard what she thought was the screeching of tyres as somebody slammed on the brakes and turned.

"Are you driving?" Julia asked.

"Jessie is," Barker called back. "If you can call it that. Can I call you back?"

"Yeah, sure," she whispered, opening her eyes. "No problem."

"Are you okay?" he asked, seeming to pick up on the sadness in her voice. "You sound – *Jessie!* You have to stop at zebra crossings! Julia, I have to go. I'll call you back later."

Barker hung up, leaving her alone in the drawing room once more. She twirled the phone in-between her fingers, turning her attention to the banquet table, which had already been set for the meal ahead. Two larger, almost throne-like chairs had been brought in and placed at either end of the long table, no doubt for the two siblings to take centre stage. Julia shook her head, unsure why she was still surprised by Charlotte and Rory's behaviour.

"Can I help you?"

Julia spun around, her heart stopping when she saw Charlotte standing in the doorway of the drawing room, her auburn hair flowing freely down her front, concealing the sides of her pale face. Despite the young woman's impossibly tall heels, Julia hadn't heard her creep up on her.

"I was just admiring your table setting," Julia said quickly, pushing forward a smile. "It's very beautiful."

"The silver has been in our family for three generations," she replied flatly, returning the fake smile.

Julia looked to the silver cutlery and goblets, nodding her appreciation of their beauty. When she turned back to Charlotte, it was obvious neither of them cared for the forced small talk.

"If you need any help with tonight, I'd be more than happy to step in," Julia offered, already knowing the answer.

"That's a very kind offer, but it's quite alright," Charlotte said as she walked past Julia towards the two large armchairs facing out towards the window. "Now, if you'll excuse me, I have a little work to be getting on with."

Julia watched as Charlotte settled into the same armchair she had sat in the day before. Julia looked back to the secret door, and she suddenly had the strangest feeling that Charlotte knew exactly what Julia had done and what she had overheard. Her heart fluttered when she realised it was more than likely that DI Fletcher had presented Julia's madcap theory to her. Not wanting to stay in the woman's frosty presence any longer, she turned back to the open doors, stopping in her tracks when she saw Andrew watching her in the doorway.

The overpowering scent of whisky mixed in with the heather uncomfortably turned Julia's stomach. He stared down at her with puffy glassy eyes, the stubble thicker than ever, and his little wisps of hair practically standing on end. She was unsure if he was even looking at her, or just through her. Not wanting to stick around to find out, she walked around the looming man, only turning back when she was in the safety of the corridor. Andrew walked over to the other armchair, where a full decanter of whisky and a clean crystal tumbler were waiting for him. Julia would have given every penny she owned to listen in on their conversation, but she knew it wasn't safe, even if she did crawl around on her hands and knees and hide behind furniture again.

Her gran and sister had left the sunroom, and they were waiting for Julia by the reception desk in the entrance hall. When Julia caught up with them, Rory appeared from the office, a professional yet unsettling smile on his smug face.

"Remember your check-out is at ten tomorrow morning, ladies," Rory said through his smile, his eyes trained on Julia. "I hope you've enjoyed your stay here."

Dot opened her mouth to reply, but Julia looped her arm around her gran's and pulled her towards the door. They set off towards their bedrooms to prepare for that evening's dinner, leaving Rory hanging.

"He doesn't even work here," Sue whispered to Julia as they walked up the steps towards their bedroom. "I thought he was a lawyer?"

"I think what this castle needs more than ever is a lawyer," Julia whispered back, careful not to catch Dot's attention. "I think I might have a theory about what is going on here."

"Let me guess, you're not going to tell me?" Sue asked, suddenly stopping in her tracks.

"I need proof. But don't worry, we're going to get it."

"*We?*" Sue mumbled as she pinched between her brows. "So an afternoon nap is out of the question?"

"You can nap back in Peridale," Julia replied as they set off back up the stairs to catch up with their gran. "You've slept like a cat on this trip. I didn't realise relaxing was so exhausting."

"Well, it is."

With a large yawn, Dot retreated into her bedroom with a promise to meet them in two hours to head down to the drawing room together. When they were alone in their bedroom, Julia explained her theory to Sue, whose jaw dropped further and further with each sentence.

"You're insane, Julia," Sue whispered, shaking her head as she slammed herself down onto her bed. "I really hope you're right about this."

"Me too," Julia whispered, her chest pounding.

Sue looked as though she was going to add something else, but her eyes fluttered, and as though she couldn't control it, she drifted off to sleep and was snoring in seconds. Julia let out a small yawn herself as she walked over to the window looking out over the castle.

She looked down at the bridge where she had shared Mary's final moments. Despite her reservations, she owed it to Mary to uncover the truth, whatever the cost. She turned back to her sister as she curled up like a tiny baby on top of her sheets. She looked so peaceful and comfortable. The thought of a nap tempted Julia more than it ever had, but she was scared of her thoughts slipping away from her.

CHAPTER 12

"*Breathe in!*" Sue demanded as she attempted to zip up the dress she had insisted Julia wear. "I can't believe you didn't bring any gowns!"

"I can't believe you brought *six!*"

"You never know when the occasion calls for an outfit change." She hoisted up a leg and crammed it against the small of Julia's back as she forced her into the wall.

The zipper travelled all the way up to Julia's neck. She attempted to relax, but it appeared she was not going to be breathing for the rest of the night.

"It's too tight," Julia wheezed, resting her hand on her stomach.

"It's meant to be," Sue whispered as she pushed her in front of the floor length mirror. "Stop complaining and be a girl for once."

Julia's reflection caught her off guard. Back home, she usually wore simple and comfortable dresses that stopped at her shoulders and exactly at her knees. While in Scotland, she had been wearing comfortable jeans and jumpers. Neither of those outfits stared back at Julia in the mirror.

"I look -,"

"*Beautiful*," Sue interrupted as she picked up Julia's hair and held it up at the back of her head. "I think we should put your hair up."

Julia looked down at the scarlet dress, which ran from her wrists, up to her shoulders, and then down to the floor. It cut across her chest in a sweetheart neckline, making her décolletage pop in a way she had never seen before. Under her bust, the dress ran tight against her body, nipping in at the knees before flaring out into a subtle mermaid tail. Gold embroidery ran up her sleeves, along the shoulders, and down the sides of the dress, contouring her body in a way that she had never seen before. Even though her sister was a size smaller than her, and it felt uncomfortable, Julia couldn't believe how well the dress hugged her body in a way she would have usually hated.

"Why do I have to wear the tight one?" Julia asked when she looked at Sue's black chiffon Grecian dress, which floated down her front in a complementary empire line. "Will I even be able to sit down?"

"Who cares?" Sue mumbled through a mouthful of hair grips as she twisted and pinned strands of Julia's hair against her scalp. "You look like a movie star. Do you remember when we raided Mum's wardrobe and played dress up?"

Julia nodded, the memory a fond one. Julia had been ten, and Sue had been five. They had paraded around their mum's bedroom, climbing in and out of her dresses while painting their faces in lipstick. When their mum had caught them, instead of being angry, she had joined in and played along. Julia hadn't known it at the time, but her mum had already been given the cancer diagnosis that would kill her two years later. She had often looked back on that day and wondered if their mum had played along so enthusiastically because she had known her days with her daughters were numbered. It was a memory Sue had asked Julia to recite to her so many times that she wasn't sure if Sue even remembered the actual day, or just Julia's account of it.

"Mum would be proud of you, you know," Julia said, catching her sister's smoky eyes in the mirror. "You've got a great job at the hospital, you're married to a lovely man, and you're going to make a great mother one day."

Sue smiled, her eyes filled with an unexpected sadness. Julia knew those few extra years she had had with their mother used to cause friction between them when they were both teenagers, but she knew that resentment hadn't followed them into adulthood, but in that moment, she was sure she saw a flicker of something that reminded her of those arguments they used to have.

"Come on," Sue said as she crammed the final hair grip into Julia's hair. "You're done. You said we don't have long to get this evidence."

Julia examined her hair in the mirror, pulling down a couple of strands to make it look less put-together. She looked nothing like herself, but she couldn't deny that Sue had an eye for fashion. She grabbed Sue's red lipstick from her makeup bag and quickly applied it to her lips. She puckered them together before turning back to her sister, who was smirking at her with two arched brows.

"*What?*" Julia mumbled as she tossed the lipstick back into the makeup bag. "Tonight's a big night. I might as well look the part."

"You look like her," Sue said as they walked towards the door. "Everybody says so."

"And everybody says you look like me, so you do too," she whispered back, squeezing her shoulder reassuringly.

Arm in arm, they tiptoed past their gran's bedroom and back down the stairs. Julia's heart fluttered in her chest, and it wasn't from the tightness of the dress. She knew she had one shot to uncover something concrete so she could put an end to things tonight, and if she didn't, she wasn't sure everybody would make it past sunrise.

* * *

AS THE BLUE SKY TURNED PINK AND orange, they hurried along the path circling the island. Julia figured out that if she pulled the dress up so that the tightest part was just above her knees, she could almost jog.

"It really is beautiful," Sue whispered, squinting as the last of the orange sun reflected off the cool surface of the water. "We'll have to come back to Scotland and actually enjoy it properly sometime."

"What's not to enjoy about solving a murder?" Julia whispered.

"I can't tell if you're being sarcastic or not."

Julia decided against answering. She hitched her dress up even further as they made their way up the slope and back towards the castle. Even though it was awful that two people had died, she couldn't ignore the adrenaline she felt pumping through her system whenever she was piecing something together. It was a thrill she never felt when she was putting together a cake recipe or serving a customer in her café.

They hurried into the courtyard and towards the secret door that led them through to the drawing room. Benjamin popped his head out of his work hut as their heels clicked against the stone cobbles, a screwdriver in his left hand and a piece of circuit board in his right.

"Evening, ladies," Benjamin said with a tip of his head. "You look very nice."

"It's for the dinner in the drawing room tonight."

"Is it Sunday already?" he asked, blinking heavily and shaking his head. "This week has been a strange one. I'm surprised it's still happening."

"I'm glad you're here, actually," Julia said as she dabbed at the sweat breaking out on her forehead. "Can you open that secret door again?"

"Don't want to chip a nail," Sue said with a shrug as she showed off her freshly painted black nails.

Benjamin turned and tossed the screwdriver and the circuit board into the hut. There was a small clatter and the screwdriver rolled straight back out again, but he ignored it and yanked on the door.

"You know there are easier ways to get to the drawing room," he said through tight lips as he dragged it open.

"We're not going *into* the drawing room," Julia said as she stepped in, hitching up her dress once more so that it didn't brush against the dusty floor. "If everything goes to plan, we'll be coming back through very soon. You can leave it open."

Benjamin saluted, a curious smile tickling his lips. He returned to his hut and left the ladies to their sleuthing. To Julia's surprise, Sue was right by her side as they hurried along the corridor. She didn't complain about the dust or the dampness, nor did she try to suggest they do something else. Her sister's silence was confirmation she felt that same thrill too, and she enjoyed it.

When they reached the door, Julia crammed her eye against the peephole, and peered into the drawing room. To her surprise, Charlotte had hired a team of servers, who were all running about like headless chickens organising the table setting and cleaning up the room.

Just as expected, Charlotte hurried in after a couple of minutes of spying. She was wearing a floor-length black dress, with red and blue tartan panels running down the side. Her auburn hair had been styled so perfectly it looked as though it had been professionally done. It swept away from her fresh face and waved down her shoulders, all the way down to her waist.

"Let's go," Julia whispered. "She's there."

Not wanting to waste a second, they both turned around and hurried back down the corridor. They walked through the open door, just as the sun drifted over the horizon in the far distance.

"Can you make sure you're in the drawing room after the main course?" Julia asked Benjamin when he popped his head out once more. "I'd appreciate it if you found Andrew and brought him along too. I suspect he's lurking around the castle somewhere."

"I guess so," he said with a small shrug as he tinkered with the circuit board. "What if he won't come? He's been avoiding me since he was rehired yesterday."

"Oh, he'll come," Julia called over her shoulder as she hurried out of the courtyard. "He won't want to miss this."

They hurried back along the path, and by the time they reached the entrance hall, darkness had completely consumed the castle.

"How did you know she'd already be there?" Sue asked.

"She wants to present herself as the gracious host," Julia whispered as she yanked on the heavy entrance door. "She's like a robot who adjusts herself perfectly to every situation. She cries when she needs to look like she's grieving, she's sweet when she's dealing with customers, and she's prompt and organised when she's hosting a dinner party for her guests."

They both slipped through the door, instantly stopping in their tracks when they saw Rory standing in the entrance to the office behind the desk. He was wearing a kilt that matched the red and blue tartan running down Charlotte's dress, and he was so consumed with the piece of paper he was looking over, he didn't notice that he was no longer alone. Julia glanced to the grand sweeping staircase, each second painfully slipping away. Her window of opportunity wasn't going to be open for much longer, but she couldn't risk attracting Rory's attention.

"I need a distraction," Julia whispered to Sue as Rory turned his back to them and walked back to the office.

"What kind of distraction?" Sue asked, looking confused at Julia.

"I don't know," Julia said with a shrug as she pushed Sue forward. "You'll think of something."

Sue stumbled forward, glancing awkwardly over her shoulder at Julia. She looked around the entrance hall as she tiptoed closer to Rory. Julia crept up the first couple of steps, keeping close to the wall. When she looked back over, Sue was reaching up to the top of the giant mantelpiece, the bottom of her chiffon dress fluttering dangerously close to the amber flames of the roaring fire. With the edge of her fingertips, she picked up a white and blue china vase and lifted it above her head. With the same force of Benjamin chopping wood with his one hand, she sent the vase flying into the ground near the reception desk. It shattered into a million pieces with a clatter, and Rory instantly appeared in the doorway.

"What was that?" he cried.

"That vase just *flew* off the mantelpiece!" Sue cried dramatically, waving her arms above her head. "It could have *hit* me!"

"What vase? Oh, *God*. That's a *priceless* family heirloom! What have you done, you *stupid* woman?"

"It was like a poltergeist or something," Sue cried desperately before glancing to Julia and giving her a fleeting unsure grin. "I'm going to *sue* you! Sue *will* sue!"

Rory walked around the reception desk and stared down at the vase with his hands in his red hair. Julia took her moment and crept silently up the stairs, sticking to the wall so as not to disrupt the ancient wood. When she reached the landing, she let out a giant sigh of relief.

Julia gave Sue a thumbs up over the broken section of the bannister before slipping completely out of view. She walked straight to Charlotte's bedroom door at the end of the wood-lined hall. She paused and stared at the family portrait once more, looking into the dull and lifeless eyes of the redheaded little girl staring back at her. She dreaded to think what the photographs that didn't make their way into frames and onto the walls looked like.

Without bothering to knock, Julia opened the door. She knew it was very possible that Charlotte had retreated to her bedroom in the time it had taken them to make their way around the castle, but she hoped for the best and stepped inside. The bedroom was empty.

Unsure of what she was specifically looking for, Julia looked around the enormous bedroom, hoping something obvious would jump out at her. The only light in the room was coming from a lamp on the antique desk on the far side of the room. Julia decided it was as good a place to start as any, so she hurried across the bedroom, stepping over Charlotte's clothes from earlier, which were strewn across the wooden floor.

The surface of the desk lacked a handwritten confession or anything else incriminating. The only thing that was out of place was a single pen, which sat in the centre of the mahogany desk. Julia tried the drawers, but they were locked.

She turned around and looked to the bed, but the box of paperwork she had seen during her brief visit was no longer there. Charlotte was a clever woman; she wasn't going to leave anything of interest on display for somebody to find. She wouldn't put it past Charlotte to intentionally clean up after herself in case someone did go snooping.

She set off towards the bed, hoping to find something in one of the nightstands, but stopped in her tracks when the door handle creaked and the door edged open. Fear fired up in her heart as she looked around the bedroom for a quick place to hide, but she was in the middle of wide open space.

Facing the door in the dim light, she accepted that she had been caught and that it was all over.

CHAPTER 13

"*Julia?*" she heard her sister whisper. "Is this the right room?"

Sue slipped inside, closing the door softly behind her. Julia's heart steadied in her chest, and she let out a thankful laugh. She continued to the nightstand and pulled open the drawer, her heart still pounding hard. She arched a brow when she saw an eye mask, a pack of over-the-counter painkillers, a book, and a pair of tweezers. They were perfectly arranged as though they were part of a show home, and not actually items that were ever used.

"What are we looking for?" Sue whispered, looking around the room as she tucked her caramel curls behind her ears.

"I'm not sure," Julia whispered back, turning back to the desk. "Those drawers are locked, which makes me think there is something in there, but the key could be anywhere."

Sue walked over and yanked on them just to make sure. She looked in the pot of pens and pencils on the desk, instantly pulling out a tiny silver key.

"Anywhere, you said?" Sue said with a smirk and a wink. "You give the woman too much credit."

Sue wriggled the key in the top drawer. The lock clicked, and she stepped to the side to let Julia open it up. Heart banging behind the tight dress, Julia quickly slid open the drawer. Her eyes lit up when she saw a single brown manila envelope. She lifted it out with shaky fingers and pulled out a thick stack of stapled paper. Deciding it wouldn't make a difference if they were caught at that moment, she sat down and began flicking through the paper.

"It looks like a contract of some kind," Sue whispered as she looked over Julia's shoulder.

"What's it for?"

"I think it's the deeds to the castle," Julia whispered as she flicked through the legal jargon. "It's hard to tell."

She landed on the final page, and her eyes wandered to the three signatures at the bottom. One was Henry's, one was Charlotte's, and the other Rory's. In the bottom right-hand corner, a date had been scribbled in the same handwriting as Henry's signature.

"This is from a *month* ago," Julia said, the surprise obvious in her voice.

"Why would he sign his castle over to his kids a month ago?" Sue asked, taking the contract from Julia. "That makes no sense. I thought Charlotte hated her father."

"I think she did, but she wanted this castle more than anything."

"So she forced him to sign over the castle and then killed him?" Sue theorised out loud as she scratched at the side of her head. "That doesn't sound right. Why wait a month, and why shoot him like that? There are easier ways to kill a person, too. Why make it so obvious?"

Julia didn't know. She had seen Rory and Charlotte reading through and signing so much paperwork recently, she had expected to find something suspicious to pin to them. She wasn't a lawyer, but the contract appeared to be legitimate.

"Rory is just a co-signer," Sue said, pointing out the small print under his signature. "This is a straight swap from Henry to Charlotte."

"He's their lawyer," Julia said as she put the paperwork back where she had found it, locked the drawer, and dropped the key back into the pot. "This isn't what we're looking for, but it helps."

"But what *are* we looking for?"

"I'm not sure, but I don't think we'll find it in here. We need to go next door."

They crept out of Charlotte's bedroom and back along the hall. Julia didn't dare look over the edge of the broken bannister, but she could hear that Rory was sweeping up the vase and talking to somebody under his breath. Knowing she didn't have much time before dinner, Julia pulled Sue into the room where it had all started on the day of their arrival.

"This is weird," Sue said as they crept into Henry's dark bedroom. "Do you believe in ghosts?"

"No," Julia said bluntly. "Start looking. There must be some more paperwork in here to explain why he was signing things over to his daughter."

Julia hurried over to Henry's desk. It was

cluttered in accounts, which Julia cast a quick eye over. She didn't need to consult her accountant to spot that the castle had been losing money every month. It looked like the business account savings were propping up everything and quickly depleting every month, which explained the skeleton staff. She tried the drawers, and to her surprise, they were all unlocked but also filled with more accounts and receipts. The disorganisation made her feel queasy. She spent an afternoon every month getting her own accounts neatly into order before sending them off to her accountant. She dug amongst the papers, but she was sure she wasn't going to find what she needed to piece together everything she knew.

Sue dropped to her hands and knees and peered under the bed. She pulled out an old sock and a book, but nothing else of interest. Julia rested the back of her hand against her forehead, wondering if she was barking up the wrong tree entirely. In her mind, this should have been easier, and she should have already been back in her room with Sue discussing what they had found.

Julia dug through Henry's bin, recoiling when she touched a rotten banana skin. She wiped her fingers on the heavy silk drapes, the moonlight twinkling through as she did. She peered out of the window into the dark, which looked down onto the stone courtyard. Sue tried a door on the opposite side of the room and walked through to the bathroom.

"I doubt you'll find anything in there," Julia called after her as loudly as she dared. "Maybe the contract is enough?"

"For DI BabyFace?" Sue called back. "You either hand over two signed confessions or you might as well put on your own handcuffs for trespassing and wasting police time."

Sue flicked on the bathroom light and began grabbing at the bottles on the counter. Julia tried Henry's nightstand, hoping it would be a little more revealing than Charlotte's had been. To her surprise, it was stuffed full of various bottles and boxes. She began pulling them out and laying them on the man's unmade bed. There was a bottle of hand sanitizer, a tube of hand cream, dissolvable tablets for a dry mouth, a pink bottle of *Pepto-Bismol*, and a get well soon card.

"He was taking opiate-based painkillers," Sue said, appearing in the bathroom door with a handful of bottles. "*Oramorph, oxycodone, tramadol* – doctors don't prescribe these lightly."

"Look at this," Julia said, calling Sue over.

"Remember when mum was dying and she constantly had a dry mouth and dry skin?"

"I don't want to think about that," Sue mumbled as she placed the bottles on the bed.

"Just *look*," Julia said. "What do you see?"

Sue looked down at the items in front of her. It took her a moment to piece together what Julia had only just figured out, but when she did, her eyes opened, and her jaw loosened.

"He was *bald*," Sue whispered. "And *ghostly* white."

"He had cancer," Julia whispered back, taking in the items again. "He was *dying*. That's why he signed over his castle when he did. That's why he was divorcing Mary. He wanted to hand Seirbigh Castle down to a McLaughlin, not his fourth stand-in wife. Charlotte said the silver in the drawing room had been passed down three generations. Gran said the family bought this place in the nineteen-thirties."

"Why Charlotte?" Sue asked. "Surely Rory would be the most obvious choice. He's oldest, and he's a man."

"Charlotte wanted it, and that mattered to Henry," Julia whispered as she picked up the card. "*'Get well soon, mate. Andrew'*, brief, but he *was* part of the family according to Charlotte."

"What does all of this mean?" Sue asked as she walked over to the door and stood exactly where the murderer would have been standing. "She would have been *right* here when she shot her father."

Sue held an invisible rifle, and shot it, her shoulder motioning the pushback that would have caused Charlotte's bruise. Julia's eyes opened wide, and she suddenly realised how wrong she had gotten everything.

"Because *she* didn't," Julia said as she stuffed the items back in the drawer. "We need to go. It's nearly time."

"*What*? I thought you said she murdered her father and then Mary to clean up the transfer of the castle?"

"I was wrong," Julia said with a heavy shake of her head. "I know who killed Henry, even if I don't know how they managed to get out of here without being seen."

Julia straightened out the sheets, flicked off the bathroom light, and then the desk lamp. She hurried back to the door, but her heart stopped when she heard the doorknob rattling in the dark. She looked at Sue, who was standing inches away from the door with her hand outstretched, but nowhere near. Without another word, she dragged Sue into the walk-in closet and carefully closed the door just as the bedroom door opened and light flooded in from the hall.

Pressing her finger against her lips, Julia stared through the slats in the door as a shadowy figure stepped into the bedroom, closing the door behind them. She was sure the pounding of her heart would give them away, even if she were barely breathing. In the faint light of the moon, she noticed the figure walk over to the desk. They flicked through the papers before they began screwing up each of them and tossing them into the bin. They peeked through the drapes, and in the silver streak of the moonlight, Julia saw the long and flowing auburn hair.

Charlotte opened a bag and pulled out a variety of different items and laid them on the desk. When she was finished, she began throwing something from a bottle around the room. Before Julia could try and figure out what it was, she smelt the petrol, her hand clenching her nose and mouth.

A match crunched across a piece of sandpaper, and a flame illuminated her soft pale face. She looked down blankly at the bin before dropping the flame. It landed on the soaked paper and immediately engulfed itself. Charlotte stared down into the flickering yellow light for a moment before turning on her heels, tossing the empty petrol bottle on the bed, and walking out of the bedroom.

The second she heard the door close, Julia burst out of the closet and ran into the bathroom. She looked around for something to fill with water, landing on a copper bedpan, which was attached to the wall like a piece of art. She yanked it off and instantly filled it. With the pan of water, she ran back into the bedroom as the flames started to lick at the drapes. She tossed the water, and with a sizzle, darkness swallowed the room again.

"What the -," she heard Sue cry, followed by the screeching of coat hangers, and a heavy thud.

Julia dropped the bedpan with a clang and ran over to the closet. Through the dim light, she could just make out the shape of Sue on the floor. It took Julia a moment to realise what was wrong with where Sue was placed in the pile of clothes until she realised she was too far back.

"*Another* secret door," Julia exclaimed as she helped Sue up off the floor. "Oh, Sue, you're a *genius*! That's how they got away."

"I didn't do anything," Sue cried as she accepted Julia's hand. "I tripped over the train of my dress. Maybe you're right about heels being dangerous."

Julia pushed back the clothes and they both

stood side by side looking beyond the secret wooden panel and down into the dark winding stone staircase. A cold draft licked at their faces as they clung to each other, neither of them saying a word.

"Shall we see where it leads?" Sue whispered, her voice shaking. "You go first."

"I think I know where it leads," Julia whispered back. "C'mon, we have a dinner to attend."

"Are you joking?" Sue cried as they both stepped out of the closet. "That *madwoman* just tried to set fire to us!"

"She didn't know we were in here," Julia said as she walked over to the desk and pulled back the drapes. "*Here*, look at this."

The items Charlotte had put on the desk were a whisky decanter, a crystal tumbler, an old mobile phone, and a pair of wire cutters.

"I don't get it," Sue mumbled as she squinted into the dark. "It's just random stuff."

"No, it points to one person," Julia said as she pressed a button on the phone to light up the screen. "Andrew McCracken. *Look*, a picture of the castle as the background wallpaper. Andrew loves this place more than anybody, even if he wouldn't admit it. Charlotte is trying to frame him for burning it down."

"Why would she want to do that?" Sue asked, shaking her head. "I thought Charlotte loved this place?"

"Charlotte *wanted* this place," Julia corrected her. "Now that she's got it, she can do what she wants with it."

"Like burning it to the ground?" Sue mumbled as she rested the back of her hand on her forehead. "I feel dizzy."

"It's the petrol fumes," Julia said. "We should get out of here. Gran will be wondering where we are."

"Julia," Sue said, grabbing her hand. "Remember that thing I wanted to tell you before we came to Scotland. God, it feels so long ago now."

"You're choosing *right now* to tell me?"

Sue stumbled back a little and reached out for Julia. She rested her hand on her stomach as she inhaled deeply.

"*Sue?*" Julia said as she dragged her through to the dark bathroom. "What's wrong?"

Julia flicked on the light, and Sue perched on the edge of the white freestanding bathtub. Sue's dress ruffled up, collecting around her stomach. She went to smooth it down, but the dress didn't entirely flatten under her hand.

Shortbread and Sorrow

"My life flashed before my eyes when I saw those flames," Sue whispered as she looked down at her stomach. "If we had died then, I couldn't have lived with myself for not telling you."

"*You're pregnant*," Julia mumbled for the second time that day.

Sue nodded, tears collecting in the corner of her eyes as a smile spread from cheek to cheek.

"I wanted to tell you, I just didn't know how," Sue said with a laugh as she burst into tears. "You know me and Neil have been trying for years, and I didn't want to jinx it. It's only early days, but I have the tiniest bump, and it's going to start showing soon."

Julia wrapped her hands around Sue and pulled her into the tightest hug of their lives. She felt their heartbeats sync up with the life between them, the emotion of it overwhelming her.

"That's amazing," Julia whispered into her sister's ear. "I'm so happy for you. I love you."

"I love you too, *Auntie* Julia."

They both laughed for a moment before pulling away from the hug. They wiped their mascara streaks with tissue paper, before joining hands and walking back through the bedroom with their hands over their mouths and noses.

"A baby is the beginning of all things," Julia said as they walked back towards Henry's door. "Not just for you."

"*Huh?*"

"I'll explain on the way," Julia said as they slipped out into the hall. "Can I borrow your phone first? I need to make a call."

CHAPTER 14

J ulia, Dot, and Sue were sat on one side of the
table, with the four new guests on the other side,
flickering candles and mountains of food
separating them. Julia made sure to sit right in the
middle so that she was directly between Charlotte
and Rory, both of whom kept glancing awkwardly at
the ornate doors every time they opened.

Julia, on the other hand, found herself checking

the bookcase where she now knew the peephole was, hoping her hastily made plan had come together in time. After a starter of tomato soup and a full roast dinner for the main course, her stomach was almost as full as her mind.

"This is all very delicious," Dot remarked to Charlotte, who was sitting right by her. "It's been too long since I've had a really good three-course meal."

"*Four* courses," Charlotte corrected her. "Well, that's if you count the cheeseboard and wine at the end, which *I* do."

Charlotte smiled politely before taking a sip of her wine. Her eyes darted to Julia, but they didn't stay for long before landing on her brother. They both shared a small grin for a moment, before glancing to the doors in unison.

The waiters, including Blair, hurried in to clear the table before the dessert was served. Blair appeared to be still ignoring Julia, but that could have been because she was rushed off her feet trying to prepare and serve nine people four courses, even if she did have help.

"I'd like to make a toast," Charlotte exclaimed as she tapped her fork against her wine glass. "As you all know, this week has been testing, to say the least.

Shortbread and Sorrow

Our family has been to hell and back, but sometimes you need to go to hell to realise what is important to you."

Julia and Sue rolled their eyes at each other, while the guests across the table seemed to be lapping it up. One of the women even dabbed at the corner of her eye with a napkin.

"Seirbigh Castle will fight to see another day," Charlotte said, raising her glass in the air. "*To Seirbigh*."

"And to Seirbigh's *new* owner," Rory said with a wink as he tipped his glass in his sister's direction. "*Cheers*."

Charlotte returned the wink as she tipped her glass back to him. Julia sipped her wine, wondering if their behaviour was only obvious to her because she had been the one to put out the fire.

"*When*?" Sue whispered quietly into Julia's ear as the conversation started up again around the table.

"*Soon*," she replied, leaning in. "We're waiting for two more guests."

Sue nodded and began tearing up the edges of her napkin, something she had done since she was a child whenever she was nervous. Julia was glad she was the only one who knew this, or else it would be a giveaway sign of what was to come.

"I think you're all going to enjoy the Cranachan for dessert," Charlotte exclaimed loudly, her Scottish accent rolling the '*r*'. "It's a traditional dessert made from whipped cream, whisky, honey, and fresh raspberries, with toasted whisky-soaked oats sprinkled on top. *Ah*, here it is!"

At that moment, the doors opened again, and they all turned to see Blair pushing one of her trolleys into the room with nine of the desserts in small glass bowls on top. Through the open door, Julia caught a glimpse of Benjamin talking with Andrew in the hallway. Her stomach flipped, and she realised her time had come.

Blair started serving the desserts with Rory, before making her way down the table. When she put Julia's on the plate, she was sure it was hastier than the others. She reached Charlotte, and her hands began to visibly shake as she lifted the dessert from the trolley. As though in slow motion, it slipped from her fingers and landed with a splat in Charlotte's lap. A gasp shuddered across the table as she jumped up and recoiled in horror, cream and oats staining her black and tartan dress. She turned to Blair and raised her hand above her head, ready to strike the child down. Blair cowered like a puppy about to be punished, but Charlotte dropped her hand and forced a smile.

"Easy mistake," she said through a strained laugh as she picked up a napkin and began to dab at the dress. "I wasn't that hungry anyway."

Despite Charlotte's backtrack, it didn't stop Blair bursting into tears. She clutched her mouth, her eyes wide as she watched Charlotte attempt to wipe her dress clean. Charlotte struggled to laugh it off, but the poor girl's eyes were filled with such obvious fear, it sent a cold shiver running through the room.

A small yelp forced through her fingers as the tears rolled down her face, causing Benjamin to run into the room. He wrapped his hands around his sister's arm, but she didn't move, nor did she look away from the stain on Charlotte's dress.

"What's wrong with her?" one of the women asked.

"She's in shock," Julia said, standing up and sitting Blair in her seat. "Blair, just *breathe*. It's not good for you to get worked up."

Blair's eyes met Julia's, and she dropped her hand, nodding her head as she forced back the tears. Julia recognised that fear. She had seen it in her sister only an hour ago in Henry's bedroom.

"Honestly, it's *fine*!" Charlotte called out

jovially. "I wasn't going to hit her. It was just a reaction."

From the looks of the faces on the guests, it was obvious they were no longer lapping up Charlotte's façade. Julia took this moment, turning to face Charlotte with a stern look in her eyes.

"I wouldn't put it past you to hit a *pregnant* woman, Charlotte," Julia called out, turning back to Blair as she did. "I'm sorry, Blair, but your secret isn't as safe as you thought."

Charlotte shuffled uncomfortably in her chair and tossed her long hair over her shoulder. The edge of her bruise peeked out ever so slightly from the edge of her dress.

"What are you talking about?" Charlotte demanded. "I've had quite enough of your comments! You didn't even *pay* for this trip!"

"You know full well what I'm talking about, Charlotte," Julia said confidently, forcing her shaky voice to steady. "I've put it together, even if nobody else has yet. I overheard you talking with Andrew. You wanted to get rid of Blair, but you didn't want to fire her because she is pregnant and that could reflect badly on you. Of course, none of that matters now, especially after what you *did* tonight."

Andrew entered the drawing room at the

mention of his name, lingering by the doors. Charlotte met his eyes, and behind her faux-confused smile, her eyes were filled with pure venom.

"This woman is *insane*, I can assure you," she said to the other guests, who were all staring intently at Julia.

"I've put out your little fire," Julia said as she begun to pace the room, glancing at the peephole. "At first I couldn't figure out why you would want Andrew back here, especially when you already had a perfectly good groundskeeper, but then it struck me. You didn't care about Andrew, but you knew what he cared about. You knew he loved this castle, and that was all he had. After your father cold-heartedly sacked him, Andrew would have done anything to get his job back, even if he pretended he didn't want it anymore. Of course, you offered him more than his job to do what he did. You had to. Even the most desperate man wouldn't do what he did for the sake of a job. What did you offer him? *Money*? A slice of the castle? Whatever is was, Andrew, I doubt she would have paid you."

"I honestly have no idea what you're talking about," Charlotte cried, laughing as blood rushed to her cheeks. "I've heard quite *enough* of this!"

"You told Andrew to get rid of Blair, no matter what the cost," Julia said, turning to look at the chef as she watched, just as confused as the guests. "But I guess you also told him to do the same to Mary. She was the only thing standing between you and owning this castle after your father's death."

"I *didn't* kill her," Andrew protested.

"I know you didn't," Julia said, dropping her eyes as sorrow swept over her. "But you're an accessory to all of this. I couldn't quite figure it out, but when I saw Charlotte tossing petrol around her father's bedroom tonight, it clicked. She sent you to burn the remains of Mary's car straight after she crashed so evidence of tampering couldn't be seen. There was something quite peculiar about the timing of Mary's death. Why let her come back to work and think everything was fine? Why send her away on *that* morning? Why *that* early? It's because you wanted a reason, and witnesses, wasn't it Rory?"

Rory suddenly sat up in his seat, after having been watching the whole thing unfold with mild interest. "What did you just say?"

"The fog provided you with a perfect cover-up for cutting the woman's brakes. We all saw her speed off that morning, but that's what you wanted. You made a public scene so that we all saw her drive off.

Shortbread and Sorrow

You waited until four new guests checked in, and I wouldn't be surprised if they were all in the corner bedrooms just so they could see. Even the police believed it was an accident, but why wouldn't they? By the time she was found, her car was nothing more than a burnt-out shell. Petrol is quite a clever move, I must admit. It's not like the car wasn't full of it in the first place."

"It *wasn't* my idea!" Andrew blurted out. "*She* made me. She said if I didn't, I'd never work again! She was offering me half of this castle!"

"Oh, Andrew," Julia said, turning back to the groundskeeper once more. "You should never have believed her. Henry signed over the deeds to this castle well over a month ago, and I doubt Charlotte was just going to hand half of that over to you. While my sister and I were looking for evidence to pin Henry's death on Charlotte, we witnessed her putting the whisky decanter and tumbler on Henry's desk, which was stained with your DNA from your various secret meetings in the drawing room. She also had your mobile phone, and the wire cutters that I suspect Rory used on Mary's brakes."

Andrew suddenly patted down his pockets and looked desperately to Charlotte. She picked up her glass of wine and took a sip, unable to look anyone in the eye but her brother.

"I only told Rory to get rid of her," Charlotte said bitterly. "I didn't expect him to go so far. I had to clean his mess up somehow. For a lawyer, you sure are stupid, big brother. I didn't kill my father, though. That's where you are wrong."

"I believe that," Julia said. "Why would you want to? He was dying anyway, wasn't he? The man had *cancer*. It was only a matter of time. He decided to get rid of Mary so he could leave the castle to you, the only heir who wanted it. My guess is he was a proud man, and you were the only one to carry on his legacy, even if he could barely look at you. Of course, when you secretly took over, you realised that clueless Mary had run the business into the ground, and the castle would be worth more to you through the insurance pay-outs, which I suspect is what you and Rory have been up to these last couple of days. Making sure everything was watertight just in case you needed to resort to that. I can't imagine selling a failing castle would be very easy, so the next logical step is to burn it to the ground and make it look like Andrew did it in a deranged act of revenge against your family. That's why you wanted him back here so badly, to be your scapegoat. Who were the police going to believe? A grieving businesswoman, or a disgraced drunk? You weren't happy enough just using the man as your puppet, you wanted to frame him for this and run off into the sunset with the money before any of this could catch up with you."

Charlotte furiously sipped her wine, her nostrils flared. Julia expected her to try and defend herself, but she didn't say a word. All eyes looked expectantly to Julia to fill in the other pieces of the puzzle.

"Of course, you're not the *only* heir to your father's castle," Julia said. "You had competition."

"I never wanted this place!" Rory exclaimed. "It's crumbling beneath us!"

"I wasn't talking about *you*," Julia said with a heavy exhale. "Blair, who is the father of your baby?"

Blair shook her head and looked down at her fingers, which were frantically knotting around her apron. Julia turned back to Charlotte, who subtly arched a brow as she waited to hear what else Julia had to say.

"I don't think you knew Blair was pregnant with your father's child until recently, but when you found out, you knew she was carrying your baby brother or sister," Julia said, turning back to Blair and resting a hand on her shaking shoulder. "You wanted to get rid of the girl so she wouldn't cause any problems to your plan, but when you realised that wouldn't work, you decided to step things up a notch. I suppose your meeting with Andrew this afternoon influenced your decision to resort to plan B."

"I told her I wasn't gonna kill a lassie," Andrew said, pointing harshly at Charlotte. "'Specially one with a bairn in her tummy!"

"I believe you," Julia said. "I don't think you're a bad man, Andrew, I just think Charlotte is a very persuasive woman. She was raised without a real mother, instead having to settle for a revolving cast of stepmothers, and a father who couldn't look at her because she looked too much like the only woman he loved. You said it yourself how much they looked alike. I'm not surprised you turned out as cold and heartless as you did, Charlotte. With Henry McLaughlin as a father, it was almost to be expected."

Charlotte sucked her cheeks into her mouth before rolling her eyes and leaning back in her chair.

"You're not the first, y'know," Charlotte said to Blair, sounding more authentic than Julia had heard her. "He's been knocking girls up since as long as I can remember. He paid them off or convinced them to get rid of the baby, but you were stubborn, or he was getting soft in his dying days."

Blair rested her hand on her stomach, and out of the corner of her eye, Julia noticed Sue doing the same. She swallowed the lump in her throat and inhaled deeply.

"I *thought* you shot your father, Charlotte," Julia said. "But when I found out *when* Seirbigh Castle became yours, I realised there was no need for you to be that reckless. Maybe you would have if it hadn't been for the cancer, but you didn't."

"So who did?" Charlotte asked, sitting up and checking her manicure. "I've been *dying* to know since it happened. Let us in on your secrets, Julia, since you seem to know *everything*."

Julia walked over to Charlotte and rested her hand on her right shoulder. She squeezed hard, and Charlotte let out a small yelp before slapping Julia's hand away.

"A hunting injury," Julia exclaimed as she walked around the table, glancing to Blair as she did. "People don't realise the power a gun can have. They can cause quite the painful injury if you don't know what you're doing."

Julia walked back to where she had been sitting. She picked up her wine glass and took a sip, making sure to dampen the sides as she did.

"Can you hold this, Benjamin?" Julia asked.

Benjamin reached out with his left hand. He awkwardly gripped the wine glass, but it slipped from his fingers and smashed against the wooden floor. He looked down to it, his face burning bright red.

"Some people are quite ambidextrous," Julia said quietly. "You are *not* one of those people, Benjamin."

"Ben?" Blair whispered, looking up at her brother.

"He said it himself. Charlotte was a terrible hunter, hence her injury from a simple rifle. You had never fired a gun before coming here, had you Ben? You had to learn your technique on the internet, and I don't doubt you picked it up quite well, which is why you decided to shoot Henry, rather than smother him in his sleep, or slip some poison into his food. You didn't quite realise how much more powerful a shotgun was over a rifle, which is why you have been using your left hand this entire time. The awkward handshake, dropping the magazine, chopping wood one-handed, throwing the screwdriver badly, dropping this wine glass. You're *right*-handed, not left-handed, but you've been trying not to use your right hand because of the pain in your shoulder. If a simple rifle can create a bruise as large as Charlotte's was, what did Henry's shotgun, which he made sure to let everyone know was loaded, do to your shoulder? Did it dislocate it?"

Benjamin lifted his left hand awkwardly up to his right shoulder as he stared down at his sister. He mouthed something, before looking up at Julia.

"You would have done the same," Benjamin said to Julia before directing it to the rest of the room. "She is only *nineteen*! *Any* of you would have done the same."

"How did you find out?" Blair asked, both of her hands clutching her tiny stomach.

"I suspect he overheard one of your conversations with Henry. It wasn't like you weren't in his room three times a day serving him his food. Benjamin had a knack for discovering this castle's secret passages, so I don't doubt he found the one leading up to Henry's bedroom from the courtyard. Those types of secret passageways were built to be easily accessed in case of emergencies, which was why Henry's was in his closet. You snuck up there to see where it led, and you overheard a conversation between Blair and Henry about their baby. You decided then you were going to kill the man, you were just waiting for your moment. You snuck into his bedroom when he wasn't there, took the gun from his wall, and you waited for him to return. You shot him, and then you ran back down the passage, disposed of the gun, no doubt in the loch, and you carried on with your day. Nobody knew you knew about the network of secret passages here. Why would anybody ever suspect the new groundskeeper?"

"He was *threatening* her!" Benjamin cried. "He told her if she didn't get rid of the baby, he would make her regret ever being born!"

"Blair got you this job here, so she wasn't going to go through this alone," Julia said, smiling down at Blair. "She was going to keep her baby regardless. She wanted to have the same relationship with her child as your mother did with you. It wasn't like Henry was going to be around for much longer. You hoped if you concealed your pregnancy for long enough, nobody would ever figure out who the father was, and you could save as much money as possible. Even if you had known the castle was up for grabs, I don't think you would have taken it. Out of all the people who lived in this castle, you were the only one who wanted to do the right thing."

Benjamin dropped to his knees and grabbed

both of Blair's hands in his. He tried to look at her, but she couldn't bring herself to return his gaze. Julia's heart broke for them both. She understood why Benjamin did what he did, and if it was her and Sue in their situation, she wasn't sure if she could say she wouldn't have done the same.

"I didn't know he was dying," Benjamin said as he started to cry. "I'm so sorry, Blair."

"Why are you sorry?" Charlotte cried. "You did us all a favour. Is this over yet? I'm exhausted."

"It's over, Charlotte," Julia said before turning to the bookcase. "*DI Fletcher*, you have to give the door a *good push*!"

The bookcase creaked open and DI Fletcher, followed by five uniformed officers walked into the room, all of them sharing the same dumbfounded look as they blinked into the light.

When Charlotte saw the uniformed officers, she suddenly jumped up from the chair and made for the door, but to everyone's surprise, Andrew stepped in her way and grabbed hold of her.

"If I'm going down, *yer* coming wi' me, lassie," he snarled through gritted teeth. "I've hated yer guts since the day you were born."

DI Fletcher handcuffed Benjamin, while the other officers advanced on Andrew, Charlotte, and

Rory. Rory instantly started spouting about being a lawyer and how he was going make them all lose their jobs. Charlotte thrashed and screamed against Andrew, but despite everything, he did the right thing and held her securely until she was handcuffed. He immediately offered his hands for cuffing.

When they were all taken away, Julia let out a relieved sigh and turned her attention back to the table. Dot gulped down her wine, and then Charlotte's leftovers, before picking up her spoon to dig into her Cranachan.

"No point wasting good dessert," Dot announced, giving the rest of the guests an encouraging nod to join her. "I must say, the spa really *is* rather excellent, because I didn't notice any of this going on. Top notch work again, Julia, my love."

Julia collapsed into Rory's chair and reached across the table to grab Sue's hand. They both looked at their gran as she wolfed down her dessert, and all they could do was laugh.

* * *

AS THE OFFICERS WORKED THEIR WAY around the drawing room to take official statements of what everybody had heard, Julia hung back near the window, sitting in Charlotte's armchair. She stared out at the loch, wondering what would become of the castle that had seen so much death and destruction in the last week.

"I owe you an apology," a soft voice came from behind her.

DI Fletcher sat in the armchair next to her and joined her in looking out at the dark loch. In the reflection of the glass, she caught him glancing at her.

"It's not needed," Julia said, shaking her hands dismissively.

"You have a brilliant mind," he said, his tone heartfelt. "I couldn't piece any of that together. The police force needs more people like you."

"I just keep an ear to the ground and an eye on the shadows," Julia said with a small shrug. "I'm happy being a baker."

"Well, you must be an amazing baker," he said as he stood up. "Your man back home is pretty lucky. Now I can see why he couldn't resist letting you run his investigation. You're *quite* the force to be reckoned with, Miss South."

"He's not too bad himself," Julia said with a wink. "Do you mind helping me up, Detective

Inspector? I can barely move in this dress."

She held out a hand, and he yanked her up. She pulled down the ruffles in her dress, surprised to see him holding out a hand for her to shake.

"I promise I'm actually left-handed," he said playfully as he glanced down at his open palm. "Drive safely back home."

They parted ways, and Julia was happy she had sensed the mutual respect between them. She felt bad for assuming he couldn't do his job because of his age, but she knew it had taken some guts to drop everything on her request and follow her down a secret passageway to wait for a confession that might or might not happen at the end of a long meal.

"So, let me get this straight," Sue said as she appeared behind Julia and rested her chin on her shoulder. "Charlotte told Rory to get rid of Mary, which he took to mean '*kill Mary*', which he did willingly. She also told Andrew to destroy the evidence of her brother's crime, and he did that willingly too. Then, Benjamin killed Henry, completely unrelated to the rest of the family, because Henry had gotten Blair pregnant, but he was dying of cancer anyway so he should have just waited and none of this would have happened?"

"I think that's about right," Julia said with a

nod. "Although, you missed out how great the spa was."

They both looked back to their gran again and chuckled as she grabbed the dessert across the table from her and started her third helping of Cranachan as she gave her statement, no doubt embellished with dramatic twists that never happened and recommendations for great wrap treatments and cucumber facials.

"What now?" Sue asked, linking her arm with Julia's.

"We go to bed," Julia said, letting out a small yawn. "We have a long drive home tomorrow. Are you going to tell her?"

Sue rested her hand on her stomach as they walked out of the drawing room and towards the entrance hall.

"*Soon*," she said. "I think I'm enjoying this being our secret for now. It's just like being kids again."

"But with tighter dresses and more murder."

They made their way up to their bedroom, and after Sue peeled the dress off Julia, she wiped off the remnants of her red lipstick and collapsed onto her bed, ready to dream of nothing else other than what was waiting for her back in Peridale.

CHAPTER 15

J ulia didn't set an alarm for the next morning, but she still rose with the sunrise, as did Sue and Dot. It wasn't long before they were fully packed and loading their mountain of luggage back into her tiny car.

"Do we need to check out?" Dot asked, looking back at the grand castle entrance.

"There's nobody to check out with," Sue

reminded her. "The entire family has gone. Just like that."

"Probably for the best," Dot said airily with a shrug. "They were *all* pretty awful."

Julia and Sue both gave each other the look they did whenever their gran said something outrageous. One of them usually attempted to correct her so she could see why what she had said was inappropriate, but it seemed neither of them actually disagreed with their gran, even if they wouldn't have said it out loud themselves.

After forcing the car boot shut, and squashing the hatbox Sue still hadn't had a chance to open, Julia turned back to the castle and inhaled the cool, crystal clear heather-scented air once more. As though the loch knew what had happened, the skies were vibrant and cloudless, and the water was calm. In the distance, she thought she saw a deer sprinting across the horizon, but it could have been her mind playing tricks on her. Despite everything, it was still a beautiful place.

"Get the car started," Julia said, tossing her keys to Sue. "I have something I need to do."

Sue nodded her understanding and climbed into the car, leaving Julia to head back into the castle. She wasn't entirely sure where she would find Blair, but she decided the kitchen was the best place to start. When she pushed on the door, she saw the young girl sitting at the counter, her mousy hair down for the first time, and in much more casual clothes.

Blair looked up at her with a smile, letting Julia know there were no hard feelings. Julia climbed into the seat next to her, and they sat in silence for a moment.

"I'm sorry about your brother," Julia started.

"I'm sorry I ever asked him to come here," Blair said with a small laugh. "I was just so lonely and scared. Henry was a persuasive man. I never should have been so stupid."

"None of this is your fault," Julia whispered, nudging Blair with her shoulder. "*You're* the victim in all of this, but you have something to look forward to. *A new beginning*. I think there are some good lawyers out there who could make a worthy case for you inheriting this castle considering the only other heirs are soon to be serving long prison sentences."

Blair looked around the kitchen, and Julia actually thought she was considering it for a moment. She shook her head and looked down at her stomach, resting her hand on the tiny bump.

"A new beginning," Blair agreed with a nod. "I

never belonged here. I'm going home to my mam in Blackpool. She's always wanted grandkids."

"That's a good idea. You're wise for somebody so young."

"Not wise enough to turn and run the first time Henry tried it on," Blair said softly. "Do you know what Seirbigh means in ancient Gaelic? It literally translates to doom. This is *Doom Castle*. I was doomed from the second I arrived here. It sucks you in with the beautiful views, but nothing good happens between these walls. You've set it free, Julia."

Blair took Julia by surprise and hugged her. When she let go, Julia could feel the tears welling up, but she forced them down.

"If you're ever near Peridale, pop into the cafe and say hello," Julia said, before looking at her stomach. "Both of you."

"I promise we will," Blair said with a nod. "I think I should go and pack. I don't suppose you're driving past Blackpool, are you?"

Julia nodded and held her arm out for Blair. They set off up the castle stairs together, both of them more than ready to go home.

* * *

AFTER DROPPING BLAIR OFF WITH HER mother, who was more than overjoyed at her daughter's surprise return, they set off towards Peridale leaving them to have a much needed conversation.

They arrived in Peridale just after six in the evening as the sun started to wane in the sky. As Julia drove through the village, she made sure to slow down and really soak up every tiny detail. Just seeing her café, even if it was closed, gave her butterflies.

She dropped Sue off with her gran. Just like with Blair and her mother, they also needed to have a serious conversation. Dot invited her in for a cup of tea, but she declined in favour of heading straight home.

When she pulled up behind Barker's car, she could barely contain her smile as she killed the engine. She inhaled, relieved to smell manure from the surrounding fields, and not heather. She grabbed her single bag from the boot and walked around Barker's car, which was now sporting a giant dent where the registration plate should have been.

Using her key, she unlocked the front door, dropped her bag on the doorstep, closed her eyes, and smiled. She was home.

Shortbread and Sorrow

She followed the sound of music and laughter into the kitchen. She walked in, surprised to see Barker and Jessie completely covered in flour.

"*Julia!*" Barker exclaimed. "You're home!"

"I am," she chuckled. "*Dare* I ask?"

"We're having a food fight," Jessie said with a shrug.

"We were trying to bake you a cake."

"But *you* said I always burn cakes."

"So she dumped a bag of flour on my head," Barker said, dusting the flour off his hair. "And then I tossed the batter at her, and I guess – *welcome home!*"

Julia didn't care about the mess. She walked between them, taking them into an arm each. Jessie eventually wriggled free, leaving Julia to wrap her arms fully around Barker's waist. He kissed the top of her head, before lifting up her chin with his forefinger to kiss her softly on the lips. Time suddenly stopped, and everything that had happened over the past week no longer mattered.

"So, how was it?" Barker asked. "Did anything exciting happen?"

"Nope," Julia said, as she dusted the flour off her front. "It was actually quite boring. *Uneventful,* you might say."

Barker stared at her suspiciously, but he didn't question her. He wrapped his hand around her shoulder, and they both watched as Jessie sat down at the counter, her eyes glued to her tablet. Mowgli crawled in through the open kitchen window and nudged Julia's arm to let her know he was happy she had returned, before looking at the flour and sauntering straight back out into the garden.

"We should go away sometime soon," Barker suggested as he rested his head on hers. "Just you and me."

"I'm *exactly* where I want to be right now," she said, smiling at Jessie who looked peculiarly up from her tablet. "Here, with you two."

"Did you bump your head in Scotland?" Jessie mumbled as she tapped on her screen. "I heard too much fresh air can actually be bad for you."

Julia laughed as she picked up the kettle. Staring out into the garden, she flipped open the lid and began to fill it with water. She caught Barker's eye in the reflection of the glass, and they smiled at each other. As Barker began to sweep up the mess, and Jessie ignored them both in favour of her new gadget, Julia's mind wandered to her sister's pregnancy. Without realising she was doing it, her hand rested carefully on her stomach as the kettle overflowed, and for the first time in a long time, she began to wonder if that would be her one day.

If you enjoyed *Shortbread and Sorrow*, why not sign up to Agatha Frost's **free** newsletter at **AgathaFrost.com** to hear about brand new releases!

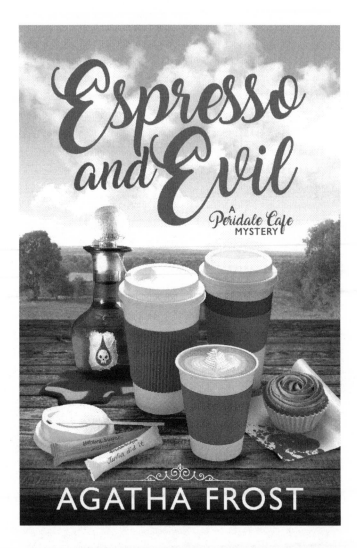

Coming June 2017! Julia and friends are back for another Peridale Café Mystery case in *Espresso and Evil*!

Made in the USA
Lexington, KY
25 July 2017